KU-650-468

Last Chance ZOO

W·J·CORBETT

Hodder
Children's
Books

A division of Hodder Headline Limited

Dedicated to Emma and Adam Finnigan

Copyright © 2003 W. J. Corbett
Illustrations copyright © 2003 Stephen Lee

First published in Great Britain in 2003
by Hodder Children's Books

The rights of W. J. Corbett and Stephen Lee to be identified
as the Author and Illustrator respectively of the Work have been asserted
by them in accordance with the Copyright, Designs and Patents Act 1988.

10 9 8 7 6 5 4 3 2

All rights reserved. No part of this publication may be
reproduced, stored in a retrieval system, or transmitted,
in any form or by any means without the prior written
permission of the publisher, nor be otherwise circulated
in any form of binding or cover other than that in which
it is published and without a similar condition being
imposed on the subsequent purchaser.

All characters in this publication are fictitious and
any resemblance to real persons, living or dead,
is purely coincidental.

A Catalogue record for this book is available
from the British Library

ISBN 0 340 86568 7

Typeset in Bembo by Avon DataSet Ltd, Bidford-on-Avon, Warwickshire

Printed and bound in Great Britain by
Bookmarque Ltd, Croydon, Surrey

The paper and board used in this paperback by Hodder Children's Books
are natural recyclable products made from wood grown in sustainable
forests. The manufacturing processes conform to the environmental
regulations of the country of origin.

Hodder Children's Books
a division of Hodder Headline Limited
338 Euston Road
London NW1 3BH

ROTHERHAM LIBRARY &
INFORMATION SERVICES

JF

B49 001 656 6
OES 428186

Contents

A Day in the Life of Ken

Everyone liked Ken, the head-keeper of the Last Chance Zoo. You could easily tell him apart by the red band he wore around his peaked cap. He also had a large red nose to match. So when animals or visitors saw a red cap and nose approaching they knew it was Ken, who would always sort out their problems and listen to their complaints.

Many years ago a child had chalked some words on the wall outside the iron gates of the zoo. The message read:

KEN'S LAST CHANCE ZOO

And the name had stuck because it was true. For it was widely known that no bird, animal or insect was ever turned away from those gates, no matter how badly behaved. All would be given a last chance to make good in Ken's welcoming zoo.

The other keepers felt the same way as the visitors about their boss. They could always rely on his wisdom. In short, a kinder and more respected head-keeper than Ken had never been born.

'Any problems?' he would ask his keepers as he strode around the zoo. 'Any small worries that could become a crisis?'

'Just a small one, Ken,' a keeper might reply. 'But I'd be glad for your advice.'

And Ken would help to solve the problem before marching away. But he was always a bit disappointed at such times, for Ken liked to tackle big problems and the odd crisis, being a head-keeper who thrived on action.

Everyone agreed that Ken was the best zoo-keeper in the world. His wife Patsy had a cabinet filled with awards and medals from foreign countries honouring his zoo work. But Ken was not the boasting type. He simply loved animals and would do anything for them.

Yet at the same time he was very shy. He would blush the colour of his cap and nose if one of his animals planted a loving nuzzle on his cheek, for he preferred to leave that sloppy stuff to his junior keepers who didn't mind showing their feelings.

Just before dawn each morning he would take a brisk walk around the zoo to make sure that everything was in order. Long before the other keepers arrived, he would be checking to see that the animals were bright eyed and ready for business when he opened the gates to visitors. Then, after his inspection, he would stroll down to the gates for a chat with Charles the night-watchman who would be just about to go off-duty.

Charles seemed an unlikely night-watchman. In fact he was a lord. For centuries his family had owned all the land thereabouts. The crumbling castle that loomed over the simple cottage he and his family lived in was a reminder of a wealth long passed. It was Charles' grandfather who had plunged the family into poverty. His passion for gambling and card-games had lost him almost everything. The only property saved from ruin was the cottage.

But his grandson Charles refused to be bitter about the past. Like his father before him he made the best of things. It was lucky that both Charles and his father adored animals, for when the council took over the land to build a zoo, the family were asked to be night-watchmen for ever. In the eyes of both father and son this was not a come-down but a privilege, for how many people were paid to look after the welfare of beautiful animals? Charles' father had been wonderfully content in his job, and now so was his son.

'How was the night, Charles?' was always Ken's first question. 'Anything unusual happen? Any escapes or attempted ones? Any suspicious noises?'

'The usual twitters and bleats and the odd lion-cough,' Charles would report. 'But otherwise, all quiet on the zoo-front.'

But there had been a time not so long ago when Charles had reported an attempted break-in, rather than break-out.

'I swear it was a black panther, Ken,' said Charles. 'I shone my torch and saw it trying to wriggle in under the wire. It could have been one of those huge, mysterious black cats that the newspapers are always reporting.'

'Well, if it tries to get in again you know what to do, Charles,' said Ken. 'Entice it in with a chunk of meat and settle it down. For no animal is turned away from our Last Chance Zoo.'

'You don't need to say that twice, Ken,' nodded Charles, turning to leave. 'And now for my bacon and eggs and a good kip.'

'My regards to Lady Sarah and the kids,' Ken would say as they parted.

Then for the head-keeper it was back to his office to listen to the weather report on the radio. Like everyone else he hoped that the day would be sunny, for sunny days equalled more visitors to the Last Chance Zoo. Later, on the small parade-ground outside his office, he would inspect his junior keepers for smartness and remind them once again, 'Remember, any problem – just send for me at once.'

'We will, Ken,' they promised.

'And should a real crisis arise you have my mobile phone number.'

'Your mobile number is printed on our brains, Ken,' they would say. 'Don't worry, if a catastrophe threatens our zoo we'll be in touch as quick as lightning.'

Then, satisfied, Ken would stride back to his office

to deal with his mail and to bark words down his hotline phone to the zoo suppliers.

'I ordered two sacks of mixed nuts, not one,' he would snap. 'And where are the bamboo shoots for my pandas? They've been sitting and twiddling their empty paws all morning. And my seals and penguins won't touch the fish you sent. When I order fresh fish I don't mean fresh-frozen, but fresh from the sea. If you wish to remain the suppliers of the Last Chance Zoo then I suggest that you buck your ideas up, otherwise you'll be on *your* last chance. And don't forget the honey for my bears and humming-birds, because we're having to feed them sugared water at the moment. Good morning to you.'

And Ken would slam down his hotline phone and make himself another cup of tea. While sipping it he would lean back in his chair and listen to the twittering, honking and roaring of his charges with a contented smile on his face. At such times he could relax and feel blissfully at peace in the zoo world he had created.

He and his wife Patsy lived in a small flat above the office. Sadly they had no children, but happily they had lots of animals to care for. There were always a few sickly creatures in boxes and baskets sharing their flat, all in need of care and attention. These patients could range from an owl with an eye problem, to a bear-cub who had climbed too high up his stump and had fallen off, earning himself a broken snout.

One particular guest was a hairy young spider who had been teased by his friends because he was hopeless at spinning webs. After lots of encouragement from Ken and Patsy he was soon weaving webs in every corner of their flat. And beautiful webs too. In the soft light from the wall lamps the webs glinted and trembled deliciously. The small spider was soon back in the Spider House astonishing the sneerers with his artistry.

On top of all that, Patsy was constantly preparing bottles of warm milk for the tiny pushed-asides too weak to battle for their mother's nourishment. But Patsy took it all in her stride. She enjoyed every moment of being a mother to them all.

When Ken and Patsy at last found time to relax, they loved watching wildlife films and playing games of Animal Scrabble. At other times Patsy would do her bird embroidery while Ken would paint portraits of their patients to hang on the walls of their flat, warm reminders of their charges.

Then, late at night when Patsy had gone to bed,

Ken would put his anorak on over his pyjamas and patrol the zoo with his stout stick and flashlight. Ever restless, he was unable to sleep until he had checked over his zoo once again. He made sure that the animals who loved the daylight were fast asleep, and that the animals who enjoyed the night were happily prowling the insides and not the outsides of their compounds.

He also checked that his charges were warm or cold enough, depending on which part of the world they came from. For instance, snakes and lizards and tropical birds liked lots of heat, while polar bears and penguins liked their sleeping quarters icy cold. Ken always found great peace during his lonely walks.

'No problems then?' he would call softly into the night. Sometimes a contented cheep or a satisfied snarl would be his reply. Then Ken would go home to bed, but never for long, for at dawn the next morning he would be up and washed and sipping his first cup of tea. Then, while most of the world was still asleep, he would be marching the paths of the zoo again, alert and ready to deal with any crisis that might suddenly arise. Afterwards, as usual, he would go down to the gates for a chat with Charles who had kept a close watch over the zoo through the hours of the night.

'Any problems, Charles?' he would ask.

'Mouse-quiet the whole night, Ken,' Charles would usually reply. 'Except for the odd screech. I've been hoping that our black panther friend would return, but nothing.'

Then, after some light-hearted talk, Charles would head home for his bacon and eggs while Ken marched back to his office. There he would make himself another cup of tea and shuffle through his papers, impatiently waiting for a new zoo day to begin. But as ever he remained constantly alert for the phone-call that could herald a problem or even a crisis that might disturb the peace of the Last Chance Zoo. Later that evening a large problem would appear in the form of a camel . . .

To Win the Love of Crusty

Crusty the camel was the latest arrival at the Last Chance Zoo. He came in the fading spring light and was unloaded from his horse box in the dark. The road he had travelled to reach this wonderful place had been a long and dismal one.

Crusty had been presented as a gift to the Queen by the Sheik of Araby. Though the Queen liked him very much, she had no room for him in her palace. So the Queen's men packed him into a horse box and sent him off to her zoo. For some reason that zoo had quickly packed him back into the horse box and had sent him off to another zoo. He lasted no more than a day in that new home. He lasted less than a day in the next before being moved on.

And so Crusty became a gypsy camel, always travelling from zoo to zoo in the hope of finding one that would take him in. In fact Crusty could claim to have been chucked out of almost every zoo in the land. But for what strange reason?

It was rumoured that Crusty's bad temper was to blame. He was said to have a nasty knack of upsetting the visitors who went to zoos for a relaxing day out. Whatever the truth, Crusty seemed doomed to spend the rest of his life on the road with no home to call his own. That is, until he was driven through the gates of the Last Chance Zoo. At last his luck had changed. For Ken was well known for giving wayward and outcast animals a fresh start.

There was no doubt that Crusty was a fine figure of a camel. Led from the horse box by Cathy the keeper to meet her other camels, he towered proudly above them. His hooves were squashily huge and his top lip almost curled back on itself with arrogance and pride. His thickly-lashed eyes had the faraway look of an adventurer who had crossed endless deserts. He was so magnificent that Lawrence of Arabia himself would have felt honoured to ride between his noble humps. The three other camels knew at once that Crusty was a camel of consequence and humbly bowed their heads in respect.

As for Cathy, she was delighted to welcome him into her desert family. She refused to go home to her flat in the town. Instead she stayed on through the night to get Crusty settled in. At about ten o'clock, while Ken and Patsy were enjoying a game of Animal Scrabble, she phoned their flat.

'Thanks for taking in Crusty, Ken,' she cried. 'I can't understand why those other zoos turned him away, for he's so gorgeous and so well behaved too.'

'Well, there were some complaints from those other zoos, Cathy,' cautioned Ken. 'But we make our own judgements here. Be assured that Crusty will start with a clean slate at our Last Chance Zoo.'

'No wonder you're known as the best zoo-keeper in the world, Ken,' gushed Cathy. 'Only you would refuse to believe the nasty gossip about poor Crusty, which shows your caring nature. And I'm certain that Crusty won't let us down. I'm convinced that he's going to make a big splash when I introduce him to the children in the morning. And I've found a lovely tasselled rug to drape over his humps. I plan to lead him down to the railings by a silken bridle to show him at his best.'

'He'll certainly be a dazzling sight,' agreed Ken, though he still sounded cautious. 'But nevertheless, I suggest that you keep a close eye on him in the morning. Crusty will probably need time to adjust to his first day at our zoo.'

'I'll be close beside him all the time,' promised Cathy. 'And thanks again, Ken. I'm certain that Crusty's going to be a huge success with the children. Good night!'

For some time Ken sat gazing thoughtfully at the Animal Scrabble board. Only he knew the truth about the Crusty rumours that were buzzing around the zoo world. Was he taking too much of a risk by giving the camel a home?

'Penny for your thoughts, Ken,' said Patsy, concerned, 'What was that phone call all about?'

Ken told her all he knew about the history of Crusty the camel. Now she too became thoughtful, and worried.

Before dawn the next morning Ken was up and about inspecting the zoo. Satisfied, he then went down to the gates for a chat with Charles the night-watchman. Afterwards he strode back to his office for a cup of tea and to prepare for the arrival of the keepers and the morning smartness parade.

It was a bright spring morning and the two rows of keepers looked very impressive with the sun glinting from their uniform buttons. Ken noticed that Cathy of the camels was excited and fidgetty. She was obviously itching to get away, to prepare Crusty for meeting his new public. Ken didn't delay her long.

'Well done, everyone. A very smart turn-out indeed,' he said, dismissing them with a smile. Then he went back to his office to pick up the keys to the gates. Arriving there he was greeted by Sam the zoo clown in his white rabbit suit. The rabbit was tapping his outsize pocket watch impatiently. As always Sam was eager to begin entertaining the visitors with his comic capers. Beside him stood Trigger and Black Beauty, his riding donkeys. After a hearty breakfast of oats and honey they were braying and pawing the ground, raring to go, to offer the children rides around the zoo.

'You're one minute late, Ken,' scolded Sam, his buck teeth waggling. 'The visitors are already queuing up outside.'

With the sky so blue it looked set to be another wonderful day at Last Chance Zoo. 'Perfect "Ken's weather",' the keepers would smile on such days. 'For the sky wouldn't dare to rain on his parade.'

Ken was quietly pleased when they made such jokes. He enjoyed an easy relationship with his keepers. It was a bonus in his busy life of problems and crises, because running a zoo for sometimes difficult animals was no easy task. He was also more than thankful that Patsy was an understanding wife who shared his burden and liked him as much as everyone else did. Probably even more.

Soon the zoo was in full swing. As the sun got hotter there was the usual rush for ice cream and cooling drinks. And as Ken strode about organising things his large red nose wrinkled with relish to sniff the smells he adored. They were a mixture of sweet and sour; of sawdust and fresh hay, fur, feather and fruit; of waters both sweet and stagnant; of perfume and sweat. But above all was the scent of excitement of animals and people, sharing this place of coming together. Though sadly in all except one place, for suddenly Ken's mobile phone began to shrill its head off. It was Cathy . . .

'Please come at once, Ken,' she cried. 'Crusty is

causing mayhem. The parents are up in arms and the children are screaming, and I don't know what to do!'

'Don't try to explain right now, Cathy,' ordered Ken. 'Just take a deep breath and count slowly from one to ten. Remember your zoo training and try to cope until I arrive. I'll be as quick as I can.'

It seemed that earlier Cathy had led her camels proudly down to the railings to greet the visitors. She was not surprised when Crusty was received with gasps and cries of admiration, for he did look magnificent in his tasselled rug and silken bridle. And then it happened . . .

A small girl had dashed towards the railings to offer Crusty a fig-roll. Crusty swallowed the gift and then spat straight in her face. It was so unexpected that for a moment the visitors were shocked into silence. Then a boy approached and offered Crusty some grapes. After gulping them down, the noble camel curled back his top lip and spat again, drenching the boy.

That second display of bad manners brought the stunned crowd back to life again. Of one accord they rushed the railings, shaking their fists and shouting abuse. But arrogant Crusty seemed well used to angry mobs. He had encountered them in every zoo where he had been a resident. As the angry adults began to berate poor Cathy, the children clustered by the railings, offering their friendly hands to Crusty and imploring to know why he had done such a wicked thing.

Through his faraway eyes the camel glanced down at them. Then, calmly and deliberately, he drew back his top lip again and sprayed them with a fresh mouthful of spit. Soaked and sobbing, the children ran back to the comfort of their parents' arms. Again the grown-ups vented their fury on Cathy, who was now a weeping wreck.

A few moments later Ken arrived at a fast stride to find Cathy slumped against the railings, breathing in and out through a paper bag a kindly lady had given her. It was plain that Cathy's lungs had been unable to cope with the shock. Thankfully, just as Ken was about to bark down his phone for an ambulance, Cathy recovered a little. Gently helping her to her feet, Ken advised her to lead the camels back to their quarters. Shakily she did so, though still in floods of tears. Now Ken, as the head-keeper of the zoo, prepared to face the wrath of the crowd, alone.

'Judging by your pompous red cap I take it you're the boss?' shouted the father of the first young victim.

'Well, you won't be surprised to know that I'm going to sue your zoo for child abuse!'

'Your feet won't touch the ground when the police arrive,' cried the mother of the small boy. 'As head-keeper, you should have known that Crusty the camel was dangerous. We can only thank heaven that he couldn't get through the railings and kick our children to death with his ugly, flat hooves.'

'Come now, ladies and gentlemen,' appealed Ken. 'Surely we can discuss this calmly. The children weren't hurt after all.'

'But their feelings were!' shouted the angry mob. 'They were viciously spat at by Crusty the camel for no reason at all. And they are such trusting little children! Who knows what damage might have been done to their growing minds? So don't try to wriggle out of your responsibilites, Mr Head-Keeper, for we know our rights.'

'We used to call you Ken,' shouted another bitter parent. 'But we've lost our affection for you now. You're just another cold and aloof official, just like the rest.'

Ken was in a quandary. He was so worried that for a moment his mind went blank. But he quickly pulled himself together. He knew that the reputation of his beloved zoo was hanging in the balance. He had always been able to solve tricky problems before, so surely he could find a solution to this one. Then a desperate idea came to him. Perhaps if he sought the advice of the person who had known Crusty best of all?

'Will you please excuse me for ten minutes?' he appealed to the crowd. 'I need to go back to my office to make a very important hotline phone call.'

'So long as you don't try to call a getaway taxi,' scowled the father of the little fig-roll girl. Then he glanced at his watch. 'Very well, ten minutes. And don't try to make a run for it because my lawyers will track you down.'

Hurrying back to his office Ken made an emergency call to the Arabian Wildlife Trust. Once put through he explained that he was Ken, the head-keeper of the Last Chance Zoo, and that he needed to speak to the Sheik of Araby about an urgent crisis concerning Crusty the camel. A few moments later he was speaking to his old friend.

'A thousand greetings, Ken,' came the Sheik's delighted voice. 'And how is your esteemed wife Patsy?'

'She's fine, thank you, Your Highness,' replied

Ken. 'And now please excuse me for hurrying you, but I've a crisis on my hands. Could you tell me all you know about Crusty the camel's early history? And could you explain about a certain bad habit he has?'

The phone call was brief. But from it Ken learned all he needed to know. As he listened to the Sheik he began to smile, then chuckle. After thanking His Highness and saying that Patsy would be delighted with a crate of figs for her birthday, he hung up. Moments later he was striding back to the railings to confront the restless and still angry visitors.

'Ladies, gentlemen and children,' he announced. 'I'm pleased to say that the Crusty crisis is solved. Now, I want all the children to gather together at the railings.'

Mystified and nervous, the children obeyed. Their parents watched suspiciously as Ken began to whisper to them. Soon the children were giggling and pressing closer to each other to form a tight group.

'Now, are my instructions clear?' asked Ken.

'They are,' chorussed the children.

'And you know what to do when Crusty is led back to the railings?'

'Yes, Ken,' shouted the excited kids. 'We'll give it our best shot.'

'That's the spirit,' said Ken, satisfied.

Then, turning on his heel, he marched away to the camel quarters. When he arrived Cathy was still mopping her tears and blowing her nose, while Crusty was sulkily chewing on his silken bridle. As for the other camels, they looked bewildered and thoroughly fed up. After a few quiet words in Cathy's ear, Ken soon had her smiling again. She was the old jolly Cathy once more as she wrestled the bridle from Crusty's stubborn mouth and led him back down to the railings.

The children were eagerly pressed against the iron bars, their mouths strangely pursed and pouting. Crusty was just as arrogant as Cathy tugged on his bridle and forced him to face them. Gazing down at their small faces he seemed unconcerned that their cheeks were bulging and their eyes were popping with the effort of holding their breath. His own eyes still had the faraway look of a traveller who had trodden the deserts of loneliness. After giving his neck an affectionate pat, Cathy stepped back, for she knew what was about to happen. Then, just as Crusty began to curl back his top lip to demonstrate his special skill, a voice was heard.

'Take aim ... Fire!' shouted Ken from the sidelines. On that command a dozen children threw back their heads and spat upwards into Crusty's face.

The change that came over Crusty was astonishing. If a camel could smile, then Crusty certainly did. He seemed delighted to have been spat at. In fact he was so happy that he hunkered down on his haunches in an inviting way. The children needed no more encouragement. They quickly squeezed through the railings and were soon tugging at his bridle and bouncing up and down on his humps. The watching parents began to smile and applaud, though they looked very puzzled. While their children played they began to question Ken about Crusty's strange change of mood.

'Well,' said Ken, modestly. 'The phone call I made was to the Sheik of Araby, who grew up in the desert with Crusty. He told me that Crusty adores children. In fact, every time Crusty meets children he always gives them his warmest greeting.'

'But why did he spit at my little girl?' asked her father, frowning.

'Because spitting *is* Crusty's warmest greeting,' Ken explained. 'He always spits at people he likes.

When the Sheik of Araby was a boy he was always drenched in spit! Of course, Crusty expected the Sheik to spit right back as a sign of their friendship.'

'So Crusty actually spat at the Sheik of Araby?' came an awed voice. 'And he spat right back at Crusty, which means that our children were spat at by the camel who spat on a royal person?'

'Not forgetting that the Sheik of Araby spat back at the same camel our children spat back at,' another awed lady deduced. 'This is the proudest moment in my little girl's life. It might even make her popular at school.'

While the now proud and happy parents watched their children playing with Crusty and the other camels, Ken strode away. But not before grateful Cathy had planted a kiss on his cheek. As his neck and cheeks began to blush, his mobile phone began to clamour. A frantic voice informed him that the chimps in the monkey house were in revolt. It was Sally, their keeper.

'I tried to part them, Ken,' she sobbed. 'I tried to stop them bending open the bars of their cage but they've imprisoned me in the car tyre swing and now I can only move one arm to call you. I think it's the fault of the children visitors. They will keep pulling silly faces through the bars. Please rescue me, Ken!'

As Ken hurried off to deal with this latest crisis, he passed a happy Crusty. The camel looked Ken straight in the eye, then curling back his top lip he spat such a jet of spit that he knocked the head-keeper's red cap right off.

'And I love you too,' grinned Ken, picking up his sopping cap and marching away. 'Remind me to return the compliment some time . . .'

Belinda Throws a Tantrum

One Sunday morning Belinda the elephant refused to come out of her stall. As a rule she was always eager to lumber out into the yard for her soapy scrub-down and nail-polish. She always liked to look her best for the visitors.

Bert the elephant-keeper was puzzled. Belinda had never caused him any trouble before. He became more worried when the two small elephants in her charge also refused to budge. It was obvious that Evie and Adam were copying the aunt they adored.

'Come on, Belinda,' coaxed Bert. 'We don't want our soapy water to get cold.'

In reply Belinda knocked off his peaked cap with the tip of her trunk and turned her back on him. The two young elephants also turned their backs, though they weren't sure why. But if Aunt Belinda did, then so would they. For their wise guardian always knew what was best.

Bert felt confused and hurt. He loved Belinda and believed that she loved him too. So why was she treating him so coldly? He also noticed that they had not touched the bale of hay that he always left in the corner of their stall in case they got peckish during the night. It was usually shredded to bits by morning.

'What's wrong, Belinda?' asked puzzled Bert. 'This isn't like you at all. I thought you loved meeting the visitors and their children.'

In answer Belinda curled up her trunk and gave a loud and defiant trumpet. Evie and Adam also raised theirs to shrill that they sided with her, though they still had no idea why she was so angry. It was also a mystery why she had forbidden them to chomp at the bale of hay during the night. It seemed as if she was forcing them to go on a hunger strike or something.

But if Aunt Belinda was angry, then so were her loyal niece and nephew.

At that point Bert lost his patience. Glancing at his watch he saw that Ken would soon be opening the gates to let the visitors in. Snatching the scrubbing broom from the bucket of soapy water he waved it like a sword and ordered the elephants to march out into the yard at once. That was a big mistake. Belinda promptly knocked the broom from his hand and turned her huge back on him again.

Controlling his temper, Bert tried the bribing approach. He hurried to his store and returned with three succulent melons. Temptingly he rolled them into the stall. But Belinda didn't even sniff at hers. She angrily batted it away for the bribe she knew it to be. Regretfully, Evie and Adam did the same with theirs. For they loved juicy melons and all things sweet.

'For the last time, Belinda,' warned Bert. 'Your bucket of soapy water is scumming over and soon the visitors will be arriving. If you have something to protest about, this isn't the time to start. Remember, you three are the stars of this zoo and the show must go on. You surely don't want to disappoint your fans?'

27

His scolding tone caused Belinda to do something even more insulting. Lumbering from her stall, she dipped her trunk into the bucket and squirted Bert with a jet of soapy water. Not to be outdone Evie flicked off his spectacles while Adam trod on his toe. Then once again the three turned their backs to show their contempt.

'Now you've done it,' shouted Bert, hopping mad. 'I'm going to report you three to Ken. Remember, this is the Last Chance Zoo. So don't be surprised if he ships you off to a circus to balance on tubs for the rest of your lives! Then you'll *really* have something to protest about.'

Fuming and spluttering he fumbled for his soapy glasses and put them on. Then he got out his mobile phone and rapidly punched in some numbers. In an instant he was in touch with Ken.

'Is that you, Ken?' he cried. 'This is Bert from the elephant compound. Something is going on here that I don't understand.'

'You mean you have a problem, Bert?' snapped Ken.

'It's more than that,' shouted Bert. 'It's a full-blown crisis. Belinda is throwing a tantrum and she won't come out from her stall. And Evie and Adam are behaving like spoilt hooligans for some reason I can't fathom. I've worked with elephants all my life but I'm mystified by this strange behaviour. Could you come over at once?'

'I'm on my way,' said Ken, briskly.

'Thanks, Ken,' said grateful Bert.

Belinda's huge ears had been flapping from the moment that Ken's name was mentioned. Moments later her hearing picked up the sound of marching boots. Sneaking a glance over her shoulder, she spied a familiar red cap and nose. It was Ken arriving in person to sort things out. But still Belinda stood her ground stubbornly. Taking her example Evie and Adam stood as still as statues beside her.

Then Ken came striding in to see the situation for himself. While poised to copy their aunt's next move the nervous youngsters counted the flies on the wall of the stall and avoided the head-keeper's stern gaze.

'May I have your attention, Belinda?' ordered Ken. 'Bert tells me that you have some problem on your mind. Well, we all have problems, but we also have a zoo to run. After the visitors have gone I promise we'll sort the matter out. But for now I want you, Evie and Adam to come out from that stall and put on your usual cheerful faces to delight the visitors as you always do. So please end this sulk, because it will only let our zoo down. I'm appealing to you as a friend, Belinda.'

'You know it makes sense, old girl,' pleaded Bert. 'Don't throw three careers away in a moment of anger. Think of Evie and Adam balancing on tubs in a lonely circus for the rest of their lives. And think of me being made redundant with a wife and children to support, for elephants are very hard to come by these days.'

Belinda rolled her squinty eyes and grunted. She seemed to be thinking deeply. Then reluctantly she backed out of the stall and lumbered into the yard, obediently followed by Evie and Adam, who still didn't have a clue what was going on. After enduring their soapy scrub-down and nail-polish they trooped across their compound to the low wall, to await the arrival of the visitors.

But Belinda still looked annoyed. It was plain that she was only going along to please Bert and Ken, who had always been kind to them. As for Evie and Adam, they were marching to the low wall to please themselves, and for one delightful reason. Unfortunately it was the reason that Aunt Belinda frowned upon, the reason why she had thrown her tantrum in the first place.

'Thanks, Ken,' said Bert, relieved. 'After all our years together, Belinda takes me for a soft touch. Your authority certainly did the trick. You always did have a special way with animals. No wonder you're admired throughout the zoo world.'

'Just mutual respect and no-nonsense love, that's all one needs,' said Ken, beginning to blush. He had given his heart away and it made him feel uncomfortable. Thankfully he was rescued by his mobile phone which began to shrill yet again.

'Ken here,' he said. 'Oh, it's you, Fiona. Is everything running smoothly in your Tropical Insect World? It isn't? All your tarantula spiders have escaped from their glass case and are scuttling at large in public places? That certainly is a crisis, Fiona. Now please stop sobbing and try to stay calm. When the visitors arrive, warn them not to picnic in the long grass. Meanwhile try to be brave. I'll be over as quickly as possible . . .' and without another word to Bert he strode away. For his part Bert hurried off to join his elephants, who were swaying in a row by the low wall, preparing to begin their act for the visitors.

'Let's make this a really good show, Belinda,'

whispered Bert into her huge, floppy ear. 'Let's see lots of trumpeting and charging around to thrill the children. And don't forget to wallow in your pond and squirt muddy water over your back. That always makes the visitors grimace and laugh.'

The wall was soon crowded with people eager to see the elephants doing their act. They were not disappointed. There were happy squeals of fear as the elephants began to rampage around their enclosure. Cries of disgusted delight filled the air as Belinda slumped into the pond and drenched herself with slimy mud. Then the cries turned to soft loving sighs as Evie and Adam offered their trunks to be stroked.

After Bert had hosed her clean, Belinda even curled her trunk around a small boy and lifted him into the air before setting him gently down again. He became an immediate hero amongst the other envious children. But the happiness and the harmony were not to last. For, moments later, Belinda's tantrum returned full-blown to create another crisis. It was then that the cause of it became obvious.

To reward the elephants the children had started to throw snacks over the wall. These titbits were half-eaten hamburgers, chips, popcorn and showers of crisps. Greedily, Evie and Adam snuffled and gobbled everything down and trumpeted for more. That was the moment when angry Aunt Belinda put her large foot down. With the tip of her trunk she slapped Evie and Adam away from the wall and then lumbered back to the pond. Sucking deeply she returned. Aiming her trunk at the astonished crowd she blasted them with a jet of muddy brown ooze. Then, nudging her charges into line, she marched them back to the stall where she made them face the wall again.

The youngsters were totally bewildered. They had been enjoying themselves so much before their aunt had thrown another tantrum. Did she really know best, they were beginning to wonder? Or was it her old-fashioned age that was to blame for her short temper?

Whatever the reason, Bert was also dismayed by her latest bout of bad behaviour. But as a responsible keeper he stayed at the wall and tried to calm the soaked and smelly, angry visitors. But his lame excuses were quickly shouted down. Fearing a riot, he desperately phoned Ken. The head-keeper had been in hot pursuit of the ring-leader tarantula when his mobile began to bleat.

'Is that you, Ken?' shouted Bert. 'I'm having more

problems with Belinda. She's thrown another tantrum and has squirted the visitors with mud. Now everyone is demanding their entrance-fee back and an apology, for being assaulted by Belinda. How do I tackle the problem, Ken?'

'By facing the stark fact that it isn't a problem but a crisis,' yelled Ken. 'Coolness must be your watchword, Bert. Smile and try to calm the visitors down until I arrive. At this awkward moment I've got the ring-leader tarantula cornered. As soon as I've snared him I'll be right over.'

'Snare him quickly, Ken,' begged Bert. 'Because I've never had to handle a riot in my long career before!'

Meanwhile, back in the stall Belinda kept squinting over her shoulder. Then she spotted what she dreaded: Ken's red cap and nose marching in the direction of the low wall. But in spite of her nervousness she was determined to stand her ground. She had made her protest, and could only hope that Ken would understand. At her side swayed Evie and Adam, as confused as ever as they counted more flies. One moment they had been enjoying the company of the children, the next moment they had been hustled back to face the wall. Now they were quite certain that their beloved aunt had lost her mind, for why else would she act so strangely and make them suffer so?

Down at the wall, above the din of the furious crowd, Bert was explaining to Ken what had happened. When he described how Belinda had lost her temper when the children had thrown rewards to Evie and Adam, Ken's genius with animals came into play. He knew what might be wrong. But first there were the threatening visitors to pacify. Approaching them, the head-keeper held up his hands for silence.

'Ladies, gentlemen and children,' he said. 'You may have noticed that our Belinda is not her lovable self today. So with great regret your favourite compound will be closed until she gets well again. But I'm sure that after lots of rest she'll soon be entertaining you once more. In the meantime Bert and I would like to thank you for being so understanding. And don't forget that the Last Chance Zoo has lots of other attractions to offer. I recommend that you wander over to Fiona's Tropical Insect World for a wonderful shivery experience. She has insects there to chill the blood. But don't be alarmed, for her tarantula spiders are securely under lock and key, of course . . .'

But the visitors were no longer listening. They were staring curiously at Ken's head. Then a small girl pointed and giggled; Ken's red cap was moving on its own. It was then that the head-keeper remembered. He had trapped the ring-leader spider and popped it under his cap, intending to return it to Fiona, who had captured all the others. Then when Bert had phoned with his latest crisis, Ken in his haste, had forgotten about the rebel tarantula. Now it was crawling beneath his cap, desperately trying to lift it to get some light and fresh air.

Seizing the moment to humour the crowd Ken went into a little act. Like a conjurer he produced the spider from his cap and let it scurry on to his shoulder where it squatted, its orange and black hairy legs waving menacingly, its eyes glittering as if looking for prey. At first the crowd gasped and shrank away. Then when they saw it tenderly nuzzle Ken's chin they began to laugh and applaud. Thus in good spirits they began to drift away from the wall to the other wonders on offer at the Last Chance Zoo. There was always tomorrow to revisit their elephant favourites after all.

Ken and Bert hurried back to the stall to get to the bottom of Belinda's puzzling problem. Ken approached and began to pat her trunk and whisper in her ear. It was uncanny the way he seemed to understand her soft grunts and sighed replies. After a while he gave her ear an affectionate tug and returned to worried Bert.

'I think I know her problem,' he said. 'Belinda seems to be worrying about the health of Evie and Adam. As their guardian aunt she's concerned about the bad habits they're picking up from the children. I think the solution is to put up a large poster outside the elephant enclosure for the visitors to read,' and then he went on to explain to Bert his whole plan.

'Brilliant, Ken,' grinned Bert. 'Why didn't I think of that? But then I'm not the best head-keeper in the world, I suppose.'

Before Ken could start to blush again his mobile phone went off. It was Fiona, in floods of tears.

'I've got another crisis, Ken,' she sobbed. 'All my tarantulas are back in custody, except for the ring-leader who is still at large. I've searched everywhere but there's no sign of him. Now I'm afraid that he'll scuttle back in the night and organise another break-out!'

'Calm down, Fiona,' soothed Ken. 'The situation is under control. But I'll keep the good news under my hat until I arrive and explain. Now please stop crying, or you'll give yourself hiccups.'

Scooping the snoozing ring-leader tarantula from his shoulder he stuffed him back under his cap. Moments later he was striding away in the direction of the Tropical Insect World.

'What about the poster and the other arrangements, Ken?' called Bert after him.

'Everything will be taken care of, Bert,' called Ken over his shoulder. 'Just try to keep Belinda and the youngsters calm until I get back to you.'

Keeping Belinda calm was easier said than done. Each time Bert stroked her or spoke to her, she ignored him coldly, which was hurtful, for he loved her very much. Evie and Adam were also getting the icy treatment from their aunt. When they cast her soulful looks she responded with angry glares. So they wisely decided to stand very still and gaze at the wall again.

Later that evening, after Ken had closed the gates of the zoo, he came limping into the elephant stall. He was limping because he had tried to separate two feuding mongooses and both of them had bitten him on the ankle. But in spite of his injuries Ken had not forgotten Bert and his worries. Under his arm was a rolled-up poster that Patsy his wife and Debbie the zoo artist had designed that afternoon. As the spring sun began to set the two got busy. Soon they had pasted the poster on to the notice board by the low wall. Standing back to admire it, they parted as satisfied and smiling friends.

Monday was a spring holiday and looked set to be a beautiful and busy day. The sun was already shining warmly when Ken unlocked the gates to let the visitors in. As usual many visitors made a bee-line for the elephant compound. It was a strange fact that most days out at any zoo began with a visit to the elephants.

Though still in a prickly mood, Belinda had endured her soapy scrub-down and nail-polish. Evie and Adam quietly followed her example. Then Bert led them across to the wall where they began to sway in a row as they always did. But something was different this morning. As the visitors and their children began to gather, a brightly coloured poster caught their eye. It read:

Please do not feed Evie and Adam junk food.
Growing young elephants need a balanced diet.
Currant buns and fresh vegetables can be bought at

Patsy's stall. Enjoy the healthy sparkle in Evie and Adam's eyes as they tuck into their wholesome snacks, all at cheap prices

Signed Aunt Belinda

Visitors to zoos are usually kind and understanding. After reading the poster many people were lining up to buy bags of buns and fresh greens from Patsy's small market stall set out by the low wall.

'Come and get your fresh veggies,' she sang, enjoying herself. 'Roll up and throw hot buns at Evie and Adam, and don't pick all the currants out!'

Lots of visitors remarked what a pretty grandmotherly lady she was. With her grey hair and her warm smile, everyone agreed that she looked very much like the Queen.

The amount of healthy snacks thrown over the wall was astonishing. The amount that the children bought and ate themselves was also amazing. It seemed that the poster had started a craze for sensible eating amongst elephants and children alike.

Ken and Patsy and Bert were very pleased. So was Belinda. She was so happy that she gave the children rides around the zoo in the special wicker-basket Bert saddled on her back.

Few noticed the red cap and nose of Ken quietly slipping away. After taking in the scene he strode away smiling. Moments later he was back in his office, barking orders down his phone at the suppliers, waiting hopefully for the next problem or crisis to occur.

As for Evie and Adam, they snuffled up and gobbled down every last bun and Brussels sprout. It seemed that Aunt Belinda had always known best after all. Though the youngsters did miss the tangy taste of salt and vinegar crisps. As they grew in size and health they always would.

The Wayne and Percy Crisis

Percy the python had a reputation for squeezing things. In fact he squeezed almost everything that came within reach of his coils. His zoo home was always a strong glass room so that the visitors could peer in and admire him without danger. His partner Pandora was much more gentle natured. But she was always fiercely defensive if Percy was punished for squeezing something he shouldn't. And that was the problem. For when Percy grew bored with squeezing the tree and the log in his home he would attempt to squeeze the kindly keepers who fed him. Though Percy had never crushed and murdered a keeper, most zoos seized the chance to get rid of him. And this resulted in the python pair being moved from zoo to zoo, branded as badly behaved and dangerous. Percy and Pandora ended up at the only place that would take them in, namely, Ken's Last Chance Zoo.

Robin the Snake House keeper was delighted with his magnificent new snakes. So were the visitors and their children who flocked to gaze at them through the thick glass of their latest home.

'I'm getting queues forming up to see them, Ken,' said Robin, excitedly. 'My Snake House is easily the main attraction these days.'

'And I'm pleased for you, Robin,' said Ken, adding gravely, 'but do take care. Don't ever forget that Percy came here with a dubious reputation.'

'I know how to handle Percy, Ken,' grinned Robin. 'He's as harmless as a mouse if he's treated right.'

He would come to regret those words.

It was Saturday morning at the Last Chance Zoo. Ken was in his office arguing with the suppliers down the phone when a lady burst in.

'How dare you sit there drinking tea and chatting,'

she yelled. 'My little boy Wayne is at this moment trapped in the coils of your python. I demand that you come and rescue him at once!'

'Which python?' asked Ken, alarmed. 'Percy or Pandora?'

'The enormous one,' the lady sobbed. 'The one with the mean yellow eyes and the toothy sneer on its face!'

'It had to be Percy,' groaned Ken, springing to his feet. He clapped his peaked cap on his head. 'And what's Robin the Snake House keeper doing?'

'He's grappling with the end of Percy's tail,' cried the trembling lady. 'And he's having no success at all. He keeps getting swung from the end of it.'

'This sounds like a full-blown crisis to me,' snapped Ken. 'Let's hope that Percy has had his breakfast. Follow me, madam.'

The Snake House was in uproar. People were screaming and children were cheering as they goggled and pointed through the glass at the tropical scene beyond. Debbie the zoo artist had proudly created the steaming swamp as her idea of a perfect python world. Inside she had planted lush green ferns surrounding a rotting log that she was certain all pythons would enjoy as their home.

But inside that exotic world a deadly struggle was taking place. For some visitors it was like watching an exciting adventure film on telly, but for the more sensible ones it was clear that a real life and death struggle was taking place before their eyes.

Waving his red cap of authority, Ken pushed his way through the crowd. What he saw through the glass filled him with horror. All that could be seen of Wayne were his white trainers and his head with its baseball cap still in place. The rest of him was hidden amongst Percy's coloured coils. But, astonishingly, Wayne was smiling and seemed to be enjoying himself. He was either a very brave boy or a very stupid one.

Ken tried to stay calm amidst the panic. He stared through the glass, trying to size up the situation inside. His gaze travelled from trapped Wayne down Percy's enormous length. There he saw brave and battered Robin grimly clinging to the great snake's tail. It was clear what Robin was trying to do. Thanks to Ken's training he was using his common sense and trying to stop Percy anchoring his tail on something solid. Because if a python anchors his tail it can increase his squeezing power, and in this case it might be goodbye to Wayne.

At that moment Ken felt great respect for his pupil. He silently vowed that if Robin came out of this alive he would award him one of the bravery medals that he kept in a drawer in his office desk. But Ken knew that this was no time for dreaming. Prompt action was needed at this perilous moment.

'Just try and hang on, Robin,' he mouthed through the glass. 'Don't let go of Percy's tail whatever you do. This is my plan. I'm coming inside to join you, to make a grab for Percy's head. Then we'll have his two dangerous ends secured.'

'How about my Wayne's head?' yelled the lady. 'I warn you, if my son is squeezed to death I'm going straight to the newspapers. Then the name of your zoo will be mud throughout the land. Then you'll be on *your* last chance, never mind about your vicious animal rejects.'

'Just try to stay calm, madam,' ordered Ken. 'As professionals, Robin and I know exactly what we're doing. Now will you please stand aside while I ask some questions? So, everyone, is there a witness who saw what happened?'

'I did,' said a small girl, shooting her hand up. 'I saw Wayne sneak round the back of the Snake House and squeeze in through the python's food flap.'

'Then suddenly Percy whipped around and seized Wayne in his coils,' shouted a boy, his eyes shining excitedly. 'It all happened so fast I'd like to see it again. Is there a button to press for an instant replay, Ken?'

'This is real life, not television, young man,' said Ken sternly. 'And Batman certainly will not be coming to rescue Wayne.'

'So is Percy going to swallow Wayne whole?' gulped the little girl. 'He was laughing and pulling my ponytail just an hour ago.'

'Don't you put such evil thoughts into Percy's head,' cried Wayne's mother. 'My son is suffering agonies inside that glass prison.'

'Correction, madam,' said Ken. 'Your Wayne is smiling in there. Luckily Robin had the good sense to feed the pythons this morning. And now, as head-keeper of the zoo I insist that everyone obeys my orders. So please stop jumping up and down in front of the glass, it's only making Percy angry. And when he gets angry he tends to tighten his coils. I want you all to calm down while Robin and I deal with this crisis.'

A stillness fell over the crowd in the Snake House. They realised that the next sudden movement could spell the end for poor little Wayne.

'I'm now going around to the back of the Snake House,' said Ken. 'And using my master key I'm going to slip inside the emergency door. So keep as still and as quiet as possible for the sake of Wayne and Robin.'

'We will, Ken,' whispered the crowd. 'And the best of luck. We'll be keeping our fingers crossed that you all come out alive.'

'Snatch my precious Wayne from the jaws of death, that's all I pray,' wept the lady. 'For he's all I've got left, apart from my cat.'

'I know my job, madam,' said Ken, fumbling through his bunch of keys. 'And I'm not without sympathy. Wayne's safety is just as important to me. So will you please let go of my sleeve and try to control yourself?'

And on that kind though stern note he strode round to the back of the Snake House and out of view. A few moments later the tense crowd spied him again. He was now inside the python's home, his red cap and red nose wreathed in tropical steam. Everyone pushed and shoved to get a better view through the glass. Ken was shouting some muffled words into Robin's ear. Shocked and battered Robin nodded and took a firmer grip on Percy's tail. Then Ken began to advance slowly towards the snake's hissing head.

In the meantime Wayne's white trainers had vanished inside Percy's tightening coils. It was clear that Ken was racing against time to prevent the boy's head and baseball cap disappearing too. And there was another danger threatening. Curled up beneath the rotting log Pandora was watching every move with a suspicious look on her triangular face. There was no doubt that she would glide to the rescue of Percy if it looked as if he would be harmed.

'Look out behind you, Ken and Robin,' yelled the children, pounding their fists on the glass. 'If Pandora strikes from the rear you'll all be goners!'

Now everything depended on Ken. If he failed to meet this crisis it was goodbye to Wayne, Robin and himself, and also goodbye to his beloved Last Chance Zoo. For the council who owned it had always frowned at the misfit and badly behaved animals that Ken took in, so they would seize the chance to close the zoo if a child was swallowed by a python with a dangerous reputation.

Ken was thinking of all those things as he finally reached Percy's fanged head, his task to save Wayne from a horrible, smothering death. All his skills with animals came into play as he gently stroked Percy's nose. Then he began to murmur strange words while gazing into the snake's slitted yellow eyes. For a while Percy glared balefully back, his fangs bared and ready to bite.

But Ken fought back his own fear as he continued to whisper and soothe, his eyes never once leaving Percy's as they strove in their battle of wills. Then slowly the snake's eyes began to droop before Ken's relentless gaze. At the same time his coils began to slacken and fall away from the tightly squeezed boy. Then as if in a dream Percy slid away to join Pandora under the rotting log where he instantly fell asleep.

The crowd clapped and cheered as Ken carried Wayne back to his weeping mother. They would have cheered even louder if she had clipped his ear for causing all the trouble. For Wayne could be a spiteful pest as many children knew. But his mother didn't clip him, but just hugged him. For Wayne was her whole life, apart from her cat.

Robin earned a special round of applause for his bravery. It was a marvel he was still alive after the battering he had endured on the end of Percy's tail. It seemed that everyone was happy about the outcome except for Wayne, who was sulking. After all, he was the one who had been trapped in Percy's coils, so why were Robin and Ken being slapped on the back while he was ignored?

'Please,' said Ken, blushing. 'I only did my job as head-keeper. It's Robin who deserves the praise.'

Bruised and battered and slapped on the back, Robin looked very proud. He had proved himself in the eyes of Ken and that was reward enough. But there was more to come for the brave young keeper.

'Quiet, please,' said Ken. 'I'd like to make a little speech. We all saw Robin risk his life to save Wayne, who shouldn't have been so reckless in the first place. As for Percy, he was only doing what a snake must do to protect his home and his Pandora. He is a nice, friendly python if he isn't provoked. But back to Robin. Because of his swift action I'm going to award him the Outstanding Bravery Medal from my desk drawer, and also put his name forward for a pay-rise.'

'Don't forget to award *yourself* a medal, Ken,' yelled the delighted crowd.

'How about awarding my Wayne a medal?' cried the outraged lady. 'He's the one who endured all the agony in Percy's coils. He could be famous throughout the land when the newspapers hear about his bravery. And this tin-pot zoo could use the publicity.'

'The Last Chance Zoo thrives on merit, not publicity, madam,' said Ken with dignity. He then appealed to the crowd. 'And now I think we should leave Percy and Pandora alone and in peace for the rest of the day. For Wayne's unthinking behaviour has left them totally shocked. But don't forget, our zoo has lots of other wonderful attractions that I urge you to visit. And the lions should be being fed about this time. Thank you, everyone, and please enjoy yourselves this sunny Saturday morning.'

'But I want a medal like Robin,' whined Wayne. 'To wear as a hero when I go back to school.'

'Think yourself lucky you're still alive,' scolded his mother, dragging him away. 'Anyway, that head-keeper only hands out medals to his friends.'

After the crowd had departed Robin spoke to his boss.

'What did you do in there, Ken?' he asked, puzzled. 'Did you hypnotise Percy to make him release Wayne and slide away like that?'

'Nothing so sinister,' smiled Ken. 'It was just a little trick that I learned in the jungle. One day I was collecting rare beetles when I came face to face with a black mamba snake who meant business. He was glaring and waiting for an excuse to attack. So I glared right back at him. It was a battle of wills, you see.'

'And what happened?' asked wide-eyed Robin.

'The black mamba blinked first,' grinned Ken. 'And slid very humbly away.'

'So Percy blinked first when you stared him out,' said Robin, now understanding. Then he looked puzzled again. 'But what would have happened had you blinked first, Ken?'

'It doesn't bear thinking about,' said the head-keeper, adjusting his red cap. 'And now be sure to make a fuss of Percy today, Robin. His pride is bound to be hurt after the Wayne episode. And I want you to look extra-smart in the morning, because I'll be presenting you with your medal in front of all the visitors.'

'I'm deeply honoured, Ken,' said Robin. 'But I'd like to say that you were the really brave one in there. If anyone deserves a medal . . .'

At that moment Ken's mobile began to shrill, thus sparing his blushes.

'Ken here,' he said, listening carefully. 'You say that the two mountain billy goats are locking horns on their crag? And they're in danger of falling over the cliff? Try to wrestle them apart if you can. I'll be there immediately.'

And without a backward glance at Robin he strode away, one crisis solved and another looming. Just a typical day in Ken's happy life at the troublesome Last Chance Zoo.

Tweenie is Fading Away

'I have some bad news, Ken,' said Sally's sad voice down the phone. 'Tweenie is getting no better. I think she's fading away.'

'I'm so sorry,' said Ken, softly. 'Patsy is here with me. I'll put her on.'

'We all did our best, Sally,' said Patsy, a sob in her voice. 'Are you sure there's nothing we can do for her?'

'I'd be glad if you could come over,' grieved Sally, 'to help me and her parents cope through her final hours.'

'We're on our way,' said Patsy, putting down the phone. She and Ken had been playing their nightly game of Animal Scrabble when Sally from the Monkey House had called. As they hurried from their flat above the office they were thinking back to a time not so long ago . . .

The two bush-baby lemurs had arrived from Africa in a cheap crate. They had been smuggled into the country by wicked people, greedy to make a profit from them because of their rarity. The long journey had weakened them and they had remained sickly ever since. The Royal Society for the Prevention of Cruelty to Animals had done their best to help them, but they finally agreed that the best place for them was in a zoo. Perhaps they would gain comfort by being with other lemurs.

But sadly it didn't work out. Every zoo that took them in was soon anxious to move them on. The usual excuse was that the bush-babies were too sad looking to provide entertainment for their visitors. The pathetic pair were finally shunted off to a zoo where most no-hoper animals ended up, and were fully expected to die there. But Ken and Patsy of the Last Chance Zoo had other ideas.

Patsy immediately took over and nursed them back to health in the flat above the office. She named them Mark and Meg. Those were the names she would have called her own children had she been lucky enough to have them. She tended the bush-babies day and night, determined that they would have a chance at life despite what the other zoos and experts had said. Sally the Monkey House keeper called often, anxious to learn about their progress. She was rewarded by seeing the brightness return to their saucer-sized eyes. Then, while she was fussing and caring for them, Patsy noticed something. It seemed that Meg was soon to become a mother. A few days later Tweenie was born.

The baby lemur was called Tweenie because as soon as she could scramble around she insisted on sitting between Mark and Meg. When moved from that secure and favourite place she would demand to be returned. Though she liked fruit, nuts and other things that were good for her, she fell in love with chocolate buttons. Every time Pasty opened a bright and crackly packet Tweenie would leap into her lap and chatter with joy.

Then one day Ken made the decision. Patsy was very sad but she agreed sensibly. And so a phone call was made to Sally. The girl was delighted.

'Everything's ready, Ken,' she said. 'Debbie the zoo artist has designed a lovely new home for them with lots of branches and creepers to swing on. In fact it looks like a little slice of Africa with its yellow spotlight to imitate the blazing sun.'

'Then into your care we deliver three healthy bush-babies,' smiled Ken. 'I'm sure they will bring happiness to the faces of the visitors.'

'As they've brought happiness into our lives,' said Patsy, weepily. 'And please, Sally, remember that Tweenie loves chocolate buttons.'

But Sally had her own ideas when she took the three under her wing. In keeping with their perfect African setting she determined that the bush-babies would only be fed their natural diet. She ate only organic foods herself, and frowned on sugar in any form, so for Tweenie, chocolate buttons were definitely out.

The bush-babies quickly settled into their large cage with its African setting. Lots of visitors were soon crowding around to see the heart-warming and comical trio on their favourite branch with tiny Tweenie sitting in the middle as usual. Often the three would perform to the crowd, leaping from the branch to swing by their tails from slender vines that threatened to snap, to the gasping delight of the children. Then one day Tweenie seemed to lose all interest. From that moment she just sat on the branch and stared at the visitors through large, sad eyes, refusing to budge. She would still chew her fruit, nuts and leaves, but her heart was not in it.

As her sadness deepened her fans became concerned. Even when Mark and Meg returned to sit on either side of her, she sank lower and lower into the dumps. Soon she was slumping on the branch with her tiny head buried in her chest. For some strange reason she seemed to have lost the will to live. It was then, one evening after the visitors had gone, that a very concerned Sally made the phone call to Patsy and Ken.

Now they were gathered in the bush-babies' sleeping quarters. Mark and Meg uttered anxious chattering noises as Hamish the vet examined Tweenie. First he took her temperature, then he peered down her throat. Then he gently tapped her knees with a little hammer. At last he gave his grave opinion.

'I'm afraid there's nothing I can do for her,' he said, shaking his head and closing his medicine bag.

'Physically, there's nothing wrong with her. It seems that the problem is in her mind. As if she's pining for something. But for what I'm not qualified to say.'

'Whatever could Tweenie be pining for?' said Sally, bewildered. 'She's got Mark and Meg who love her, as we all do. She eats the best quality fruit and nuts. And the visitors and their children love her. So what could she be pining for?'

'Who can say?' shrugged Hamish. 'I've got no idea what goes on inside Tweenie's head. It's a worrying problem. She might live another day, but I'm afraid no longer than that.'

Even Ken, who was usually good at solving problems, was at a loss. He had always prided himself on knowing his animals as well as he knew himself. Yet here was Tweenie fading away and he didn't know what to do. He felt almost ashamed of the red peaked cap he wore so proudly. Glancing at Mark and Meg he fancied he saw reproach in their anxious eyes. As if they believed Ken was letting them down, uncaring. And all the while their tiny child drooped more listlessly between them.

Then sad-faced Hamish departed to attend to his other patients, leaving Ken, Patsy and Sally to ponder the fate of poor Tweenie. Tearfully, Sally suggested that they should make her comfortable in a warm box to doze away her remaining hours until death. But Ken was having none of it.

'No, Sally,' he said. 'If Tweenie must die then she'll do so sitting on the branch between Mark and Meg, with the sunshine on her face. And don't forget her child fans, they'll want to say goodbye.'

'You're right, Ken,' wept Sally. 'Tweenie must not meet her end alone. Everyone needs company at that time in their lives.'

'I'm still wondering what could be troubling Tweenie,' mused Patsy. 'Having helped to raise her I'm sure that I should know. Hamish said that she seemed to be pining for something, but what? And twice she has held out her paw to me, but why?'

'Anyway,' murmured Ken to Sally, patting her shoulder, 'nurse Tweenie through the night. Hopefully I'll see all four of you in the morning, for all's not lost while Tweenie still draws breath.'

Later that night, Ken and Patsy talked about the pain of losing friends. Patsy in particular was deeply distressed. After Ken had left on his midnight patrol of the zoo, Patsy went to bed and lay awake for a long time. How had they failed Tweenie, she pondered.

She was fit and well according to Hamish, so why was she fading away? Still puzzled, Patsy fell asleep at last. In the morning she would wake to puzzle again.

When Ken opened the gates that morning the waiting crowd was buzzing. The rumour was that Tweenie the tiny bush-baby was on her death bed and fading away fast. Soon there was a jostling crush of children and parents gazing through the wire of the bush-babies' pen, many of them weeping. All eyes were on the branch where Mark and Meg sat with Tweenie in between them.

The tiny lemur looked even more ill and droopy than she had yesterday. It was as much as Mark and Meg could do to stop her toppling from the branch to the cold, hard floor below. Tweenie's huge eyes were now staring vacantly at nothing. As the children clung to each other and sobbed; as Sally fought back her own tears something extraordinary happened . . .

'Excuse me . . . excuse me please,' came a polite voice from the back of the crowd. As the visitors turned to look, their ranks quickly parted. For it was Patsy, gently pushing her way to the front. People made way because she looked astonishingly like the Queen with her lovely grey hair and warm smile.

Moments later Patsy was standing close to the mesh of the cage and calling through.

'Hello, Tweenie, it's Patsy,' she said softly. Then she held up her hand. In it was a brightly coloured packet that crackled as she squeezed it. At the sound of her voice and the sight of the packet, Tweenie's eyes widened and shone with hope. As Patsy pushed the packet through the wire, the small bush-baby leapt down from the branch to snatch it. Back on her perch she eagerly tore it open and began to chomp down the gift of chocolate buttons, her chirrups of delight bringing relief and laughter to the crowd of watchers.

Seeing their daughter spring back to life Mark and Meg began to chatter their joy and swing by paw and tail from every twig and branch in their home. Sally wept openly with happiness. Then, smiling and waving, Patsy made her way back through the cheering crowd to return to the flat above the office. For she had lots of other sick and distressed creatures to attend to.

'Well, who'd have thought it?' sighed Sally as she strolled down to close the gates with Ken, at the end of the day. 'Who would have believed that a packet of chocolate buttons would have brought Tweenie back from the depths of despair?'

'I wouldn't have expected it,' agreed Ken, shaking his head. 'But then Patsy has always surprised me with her practical solutions to problems. She knew exactly what Tweenie needed to perk her up.'

'But *chocolate buttons*, Ken?' said Sally, pretending to be shocked. 'It's hardly a proper diet for a growing bush-baby.'

'I suppose we all need a few treats to comfort us through life,' grinned Ken. 'And in this case they certainly did the trick. It did more good than harm I'd say.'

'Tell me, Ken,' said Sally, mischievously, 'people around the world say that you're the best head-keeper in the world. So would that make your wife Patsy the brains behind the best head-keeper in the world?'

'She has her brilliant moments,' admitted Ken, beginning to blush. 'Though Patsy and I prefer to call ourselves a partnership.'

'A personal question, Ken,' said Sally, intrigued. 'When and how did you and Patsy meet to begin your life partnership?'

'In a jungle, actually,' said Ken, his neck and ears glowing as red as his cap. 'I was hunting rare beetles and Patsy was netting exotic butterflies.'

'In the exact same bit of jungle?' said Sally, amazed. 'That must have been fate, Ken. And did your insect nets clash as you met amongst the ferns? Did your eyes lock together in a mesh of love forever? How romantic it must have been.'

Ken was now squirming with embarrassment. Thankfully he was saved from further questions by the shrilling of his mobile phone. After listening a while he spoke a few quiet words to the person on the other end. The call finished, he turned back to Sally.

'I'm afraid I must dash,' he apologised. 'There's a problem arisen that could well become a crisis. The lions have cornered their keeper in the cage and he can't escape. In the meantime, Sally, keep a close eye on Tweenie and don't forget to feed her a ration of chocolate buttons every day. Now I must get back to my office to hunt out my lion-taming chair . . .'

And straightening his cap he strode away to enter the fray. As he departed Sally was reminded of someone she knew well. Ken looked just like her father who also marched about swiftly, who also wore a red-peaked cap and had a large red nose. He was a bluff man who blushed too when asked questions that he thought were too personal. But Sally's father was a

mere army general, while Ken was easily the best
head-keeper in the world . . .

Ken's Personal Crisis

Lots of people knew that creepy Stan was after Ken's job. Though Stan worked in a posh zoo he lusted for fame, and the most famous zoo in the world was the Last Chance Zoo, with its head-keeper, Ken. So Stan was determined somehow to take Ken's job and become famous himself. If Ken knew of Stan's ambitions he kept it to himself, for fame meant nothing to him. Anyway, he was much too busy keeping his zoo in tip-top shape to listen to the rumours about Stan's cunning plans to oust him.

Then one summer day Stan wrote a smarmy letter to the council, who owned the Last Chance Zoo. It read:

Dear honourable sirs and madams,

I would humbly like to apply for a job as a keeper at your superb zoo. Though I am the deputy head-keeper of a famous zoo quite near to where the Queen lives, I would jump at the chance to work under Ken, the best head-keeper in the world.

I am quite prepared to start at the bottom, just for the honour of working with Ken. I would eagerly do all the lowly tasks like mucking out the hippos, or scrubbing the parrot cages. All I wish to do is to work with Ken in the hope that some day his wisdom and magic with animals will rub off on me, a very humble learner.

Please tell Ken how deeply I admire him. In my worthless opinion he is the master of zoo-keepers. In my time I have shaken hands with Her Majesty the Queen,

but shaking hands with Ken has always been
my dream.

Yours very humbly,
    Stan

The chairman of the council was so impressed by
Stan's letter that he offered him a job immediately. As
deputy head-keeper to Ken, no less. Because Stan had
shaken hands with the Queen there would be no
mucking out of hippos for him. He would begin his
career at the Last Chance Zoo almost at the top
already. When the chairman phoned Ken to tell him
the news Ken couldn't talk or hear too well. This was
because the zoo was in full swing with lots of chirping
and bellowing, radios blaring as the happy visitors
added their bit to the bedlam that was the Last
Chance Zoo.

'Ken,' yelled the chairman, above the din. 'We've
just appointed a deputy head-keeper to serve below
you. His name is Stan and he's eager to work with
you.'

'A deputy?' a puzzled Ken shouted back. 'I've
never needed a deputy before. And the name Stan
seems to ring a bell, but never mind. So long as he's

keen and loves animals I'm sure we'll get along.'

'Ken, you'll be proud to know that your new deputy has shaken hands with Her Majesty the Queen,' bawled the chairman. 'And his last post was at the famous zoo quite near to where the Queen lives. What do you think about that, Ken?'

'I'm very impressed,' said Ken, hurriedly. 'And I'll look forward to meeting Stan when I have the time. But I've got a problem looming at the moment. Eric the ostrich has leapt his fence and is chasing and kicking the children—' and then the chairman's phone went dead.

Ken wasn't being rude. He was simply too busy running his zoo to chat with chairmen who gushed about deputy head-keepers who had shaken hands with the Queen. He had his gates to open every morning, and a bustling swarm of visitors to please. Then he needed to make angry phone calls to the zoo suppliers who never seemed to buck their ideas up. And all the time Ken had to find time to pat his young keepers on the back and praise them for their dedication and effort. In other words, Ken had to create order from disorder in the wonderful zoo world he loved.

It was late that day when Ken met and shook hands

with his new deputy. He noticed that Stan's eyes slid around a lot, and never once met his own. He also observed that Stan's hand shake was limp and damp. He was instantly reminded of the giant toad who lived in Tracy's Waterworld Attraction. But Ken resisted the urge to dislike Stan at this first meeting, for he was always prepared to think the best of people before he made a judgement.

'I'm so honoured to meet you, Ken,' gushed Stan. 'Would you mind if I simply followed you around for my first couple of days? Only I've loads to learn and there's so much you can teach me. I've always dreamed of treading in your footsteps, Ken. I won't be a nuisance, I promise.'

'You're too modest, Stan,' smiled Ken. 'After working in that famous zoo down south, you must be very experienced.'

'Well, I did bow and shake hands with the Queen,' said Stan with an oily smirk. 'And Her Majesty did remark that I must know a lot about animals. And her husband seemed very interested. He asked me if I knew a lot about toads. They were very gracious to me, considering my lowly status, Ken.'

'Well, Stan,' said Ken, 'I'm sure there's little I can teach you. So perhaps you should just wander around the zoo on your own, getting to know the animals and their keepers. In that way you'll learn just how our Last Chance Zoo is run.'

'Do you mean I can go where I want, when I want, Ken?' said Stan, delighted. 'Without needing to ask your permission?'

'Consider yourself free-range, Stan,' said Ken. 'Just remember to ring me at once if a problem or a crisis should arise.'

'I will, Ken,' said Stan, humbly bowing his head. 'Thanks for trusting me so completely on my first day as your deputy. I'll get to work at once. I'm dying to meet all the last chance animals and their dedicated keepers.'

But Ken was barely listening. As Stan slid out through the office door he was already punching numbers and barking down his hotline phone to the suppliers. They were told in no uncertain terms that goats ate thistles not whistles that stuck in their throats. Someone obviously didn't know how to spell. Before ringing off he warned the suppliers to sort themselves out, otherwise they could forget about any future custom from the Last Chance Zoo. Indeed, this was *their* very last chance, he threatened.

It was on the second day of Stan's deputyship that

gossip began to spread amongst the keepers. It was plain to them all that Stan was beginning to put on lofty airs and graces. He was getting very much above himself, they fumed.

'The cheek of that Stan,' said angry Cathy of the camels. 'How dare he wear a red band around his cap? Only Ken's allowed to do that. My Crusty spat at him this morning, and it wasn't because he liked him. In fact he spat on Stan's boots which means, "I hate you very much".'

'And Stan is so toadying,' shivered Tracy of Waterworld. 'Only toads should behave like that, never deputy head-keepers.'

'Have you seen him stride along the zoo paths as if he were Ken?' cried outraged Sally. 'And not once has he tossed a chocolate button to Tweenie.'

'Stan's nasty remarks are proof of the man,' growled old Bert of the elephants. 'He had the nerve to say that Ken hid all his grey hair under his cap. Well, I've got no hair at all, but it doesn't mean that I should retire.'

'I could have smacked Stan's face,' fumed Fiona of the tarantulas. 'How dare he hint that Ken's red nose is caused by drinking too much beer?'

'Stan's plan is becoming clear,' frowned Robin, the

snake-keeper. 'He's trying to elbow Ken aside and become the head-keeper of our Last Chance Zoo himself. Can you imagine him with his shifty eyes trying to out-stare Percy my python?'

'I suggest that we take our suspicions to Ken himself,' said Cathy, firmly. 'It's obvious he can't see what going on under his very nose. He's too trusting, that's Ken's trouble. He just strides around in his old routine, the same old Ken as usual. It's as if Stan is invisible to him.'

All the keepers agreed that Cathy's idea was a good one. So at lunchtime, when most of the visitors were enjoying picnics on the grass, they went together to Ken's office and rapped on the door. To their surprise it was opened by Patsy. She looked rather worried.

'Is it important, dears?' she asked. 'Only Ken's come down with a nasty cold and he's not feeling too good. I'm trying to persuade him to have a couple of days off.'

'Then we won't disturb him, Patsy,' said Sally, firmly, 'Our business will wait for a day or two. Please tell him that we hope he gets better soon.'

'Only we're a bit worried about Stan,' said Robin, impulsively. 'And we'll be very glad when Ken is back in charge.'

'If you're worried about the running of the zoo, Ken did say something,' said Patsy, smiling a secret smile. 'He said that as Stan is so experienced he can safely leave the zoo in his capable hands for a while.'

Filled with foreboding, the keepers hurried back to their departments, all believing that with Ken away there would soon be big trouble with Stan. They were right.

When Stan heard that he was now in charge he really began to throw his weight about. The keepers could have sworn that his red peaked cap was now twice as tall as Ken's as he strutted through the zoo.

He was soon bawling them out for mistakes they hadn't made. When they protested he angrily told them to watch their tongues or face the sack. They were also shocked to notice that he was wearing a row of bravery and merit medals on his tunic that he had obviously stolen from Ken's desk drawer.

'I'm the top-dog around here now,' he boasted. 'And if any of you whipper-snapper keepers want to argue, then you know where the gates are. And if you're hoping that Ken will return to duty, think again. He's old and he's got a bad cold that could get worse, and I intend to have a word with the chairman of the council about your precious Ken's early retirement. Now get back to work! I want to see this zoo running like clockwork in case an important visitor like the Queen should drop in for a quick inspection. She always travels with a case of proper medals, not these cheap things that Ken dishes out. And I've set my sights on winning a proper medal, so get cracking!'

The miserable keepers could only obey. They returned to tending and grooming their animals and smiling at the visitors. But it was with heavy hearts. How they yearned for Ken to arise from his sick-bed and take charge once again. How they hated Stan who lorded it over their beloved zoo like a petty dictator. And there was worse to come.

'Keep off the grass!' yelled Stan at the startled visitors. 'It isn't neatly mown for you to lounge around on. From now on all picnics are banned. And so is this habit of bringing your own sandwiches from home. If you must eat then you can buy all the food you want from my snack stalls at reasonable prices. I'll introduce myself, my name is Stan and I demand that you respect this zoo as a place of study, and not a place for frivolity. This means that all noisy and boisterous children will be thrown out and banned for life.'

'You can't do that!' yelled the furious parents. 'Ken always allowed us to eat our own sandwiches on the grass. And he knew that children are natural nuisances. He always turned the other cheek when they got out of order.'

'Well, Ken's not in charge any more, *I* am,' shouted Stan, tapping his chest medals. And then he marched away so haughtily that he almost fell over backwards trying to keep his posture ram-rod stiff.

But it was not only the keepers and the visitors that Stan was upsetting. The animals in the zoo were getting restive too. Used to Ken's kindness, Stan's bullying manner was making them nervous. Instead of Ken's soothing talk and pats, they had to endure Stan's rubber-gloved hands forcing them to open their jaws and beaks, and checking their mouths for germs. He also examined their paws, claws or hooves for rot as if they were loathsome lepers.

And he did all this while the visitors were watching, which was shaming for the proud creatures. Even when the gates were closed for the night there was no rest from Stan. Ordering the weary keepers to follow him, he toured the zoo to weed out the creatures he didn't like. Armed with a long cane he pointed out various animals.

'That swearing parrot,' he ordered, 'get rid of it. I won't have bad language in my zoo. And the ostrich that keeps leaping its fence and kicking passers-by, he's another for the chop. And that one-eyed walrus is hardly a pretty sight, so he can go too. In fact I want all the old, sickly and badly behaved animals to be put down mercifully by Hamish the zoo vet. I intend to make a brand new start as the head-keeper of this zoo. Only sane and healthy animal specimens will be given a home here. I won't have the Queen offended by third-rate animals when she comes to give me a proper medal, instead of Ken's cheap trash from his desk drawer. And a final warning, I'll be weeding out you keepers if you don't come up to scratch. As Ken's retirement through ill health becomes more likely, I demand that you all obey my every word.'

'Excuse me, Stan,' said angry Robin. 'But you seem to have missed the point about our Last Chance Zoo. We don't turn away or put down animals because they're not perfect, we nurture them. We encourage them to fit into our family, to develop their personalities, to become loved by the visitors for what they are and not what they look like.'

The keepers nodded angrily and broke into loud applause, for Robin had spoken for all. This infuriated Stan even more. He glared at brave Robin.

'For a start, don't call me Stan,' he shouted. 'I'm Mr Head-Keeper to you. Or I will be as soon as Ken has vanished from the scene! And then, when I'm totally in charge, the first thing I'll do is to sack *you*.'

And he strutted away to the luxury caravan he had brought with him, slamming the door loudly on the voices of the protesting keepers, and on the bleats, the cheeps and the roars of the animals as darkness fell. There would be no midnight patrol from Stan, no words of comfort from the man that everyone had come to hate. For in truth, Stan had never liked animals much. He was in love with himself and totally obsessed with becoming famous like Ken. He had no idea that first he needed to be respected by animals and keepers alike.

As the small group of keepers left the zoo for their homes in the town they were armed with a vow, that the next morning they would take a united stand against Stan and the misery he was causing.

The zoo now deserted, there was no one to see a figure emerge from the office door. It wore an anorak over pyjamas and carried a stick and a torch. Moments later it was swallowed up by the darkness of the Last Chance Zoo.

The next morning the zoo was on strike, including the visitors. As Stan flung open the gates he was greeted by jeers from the crowd outside. One little girl whose picnic Stan had spoiled the previous day was waving a placard which read:

WE WANT KEN – KINDLY KEN NOT THAT GRUMPY STAN

Sam the White Rabbit was sitting on the ground, his paws crossed stubbornly across his chest. There would be no comic turns from him that morning. Beside him lay Trigger and Black Beauty, his donkeys. They would be giving no rides to the children until the problem of the hated Stan was sorted out. In the meantime, Stan was absolutely livid with rage. Behind him stood the keepers, looking nervous but defiant. Then Sally stepped forward to confront Stan bravely. Her words were rewarded by a huge cheer from the crowd as she looked him straight in the eye.

'As spokesperson, I must warn you, Stan,' she said. 'Because of your unkind behaviour this zoo is facing melt-down. The birds are refusing to stir from their nesting boxes, the hippos won't surface from their muddy pond and the monkeys have refused to get up to their tricks to make the visitors laugh. The rest of the animals are also protesting in their various ways.'

'And we keepers are firmly protesting with them,' shouted defiant Robin.

'While we visitors are firmly protesting outside,' yelled the crowd. 'Until we get our old rights back, like being allowed to bring our own sandwiches to enjoy picnics on the grass, and the children being free to make nuisances of themselves as all normal children do. In other words we want our kindly Ken back!'

'Well, you can't have him back,' bawled furious Stan. 'I'm in charge now. *I* make the rules and *you* obey them.'

'Not for much longer,' cried the parents. 'Because when we left the zoo last night we went to see a person in high authority and put our complaints to him. We also reminded him that we voted him into office, and we could vote him out with our ballot-box power.'

'And who would that person be?' asked Stan, frightened now.

'The chairman of the council, no less,' came the

triumphant reply. 'And he promised to right all the wrongs you've done to our Last Chance Zoo. In fact, here he comes now in his posh car.'

Everyone turned to watch the Rolls Royce gliding up the drive. Out of it stepped a portly man with a worried look on his sweaty face. The chairman had come in person to repair the damage that Stan had done to the reputation of the zoo. Seizing her chance, the little girl with the 'Kindly Ken' banner nipped forward to thrust it into the chairman's hand. So the chairman became a proper protester against the tyranny of Stan. Waving the message in Stan's face he made it plain where his loyalties and his votes lay.

'Stan,' he said, sternly. 'By popular demand I'm afraid you'll have to go. I've got no choice but to sack you immediately.'

'But sir, I was just beginning to whip this zoo into shape,' said Stan, astonished.

'Yes, your cruel shape,' cried Sally. 'Certainly not Ken's!'

'So don't think you'll get another chance, grumpy Stan,' yelled the little girl. 'Only the animals are allowed to make a fresh start here.'

'So you know where the gates are, Stan,' shouted Robin, pointing. 'The same gates that you would have thrown me out of when you vowed to sack me!'

'Take your sacking like a man, Stan,' roared the crowd. 'After just a couple of days we're fed up with your grumpy moods. Just get on your bike and go.'

Though Stan had no bike, he did have a luxury caravan. White-faced with rage he hurried to where it was parked. Hitching it up to his car he sped out through the gates past the jeering crowd and vanished in a cloud of dust. He was not seen or heard of ever again.

He was soon followed by the fat chairman. His good deed for the day done, he smiled and waved at his happy voters as he glided away in his shiny Rolls Royce. Then all at once a gladdening sight was spied. Everyone began to cheer as the familiar figure of Ken came marching from the direction of his office. He looked very fit, considering that he was supposed to be ill in bed.

'What are you doing here, Ken?' scolded Sally. 'Patsy said you were ill.'

'Oh, it was just a snuffling cold,' smiled Ken. 'I feel much better being up and about and seeing what you keepers are getting up to. So where's Stan? And why are the visitors cheering and waving banners with my name on them? Will someone please explain what's been going on?'

'Stan has just gone, Ken,' said happy Robin. 'And so has the chairman of the council, who sacked him on the spot for trying to ruin our Last Chance Zoo!'

'Stan has been sacked?' said Ken, trying to look surprised. 'That's strange. I had a phone call from the chairman last night. He said that he had been invaded by some angry voters protesting about the running of our zoo. Poor Stan, I hoped that he might have fitted in with our way of doing things. Did he upset everyone?'

'Oh, we hated him, Ken,' shuddered Sally. 'And so did the animals and birds. And so did the visitors; you can see them protesting outside the gates in sympathy with us.'

'So you and the visitors solved the Stan problem yourselves,' grinned Ken, looking very pleased and proud. 'I really don't know what to say.'

'But *we* do, Ken,' cried the children outside the gates. 'First of all we say welcome back, and now can we come inside and enjoy ourselves as we always have? And will we be rewarded for winning the fight against grumpy Stan? Our starving mouths are your responsibility, Ken.'

'You expect a reward?' frowned Ken. Then he smiled. 'Well, perhaps we can allow you one free hot-dog and ice cream each, but don't come too often because . . .'

The rest of his words were drowned out by the cheers of the children as they charged through the gates to storm the hot-dog and ice cream stalls. Then, with fists stuffed full, they ran back to climb aboard Trigger and Black Beauty for rides around the zoo, with Sam the happy White Rabbit cavorting comically before them.

'Oh, Ken,' said Sally, tears in her eyes. 'What would we do without you? Your appearance was like a ray of sunshine after the dark clouds of Stan. If there's anything we keepers can do . . . like run and buy some Lemsips for your cold . . .'

'There *is* something you can all do,' said Ken, beginning to blush at such praise. 'You can get back to your departments and get our zoo running like clockwork again. For the show must go on. And one more thing, let's have lots of smiles. Our job at the Last Chance Zoo is to spread happiness, not gloom . . .' and then his mobile phone began to ring. The keepers craned close to hear. Their eavesdropping told them that it was the chairman on the line.

'Everything is back to normal, and the visitors are streaming in, so don't worry,' said Ken. 'Now, if you don't mind, Mr Chairman, I've got a zoo to run . . .' and off he marched back to his office. Though he did wink at the keepers before he left.

'That cunning old Ken,' grinned Robin, admiringly. 'I'll bet he knew that Stan was a threat to our zoo the moment he arrived. He also knew that Stan was after his job as head-keeper. So he gave Stan free rein to rule the roost while he went to bed with a cold—'

'But the strutting cock Stan didn't crow this morning,' chuckled Bert of the elephants. 'And when the chairman called he lost more feathers than I'm losing hairs.'

'In other words, Stan cooked his own goose,' giggled Sally. 'He thought he was clever but Ken was cleverer.'

'Yes, well, let's get our zoo back on the road as Ken asked,' said Robin, briskly. 'I've got Percy the python to keep an eye on in case he gets too loving and tries to hug another child to death.'

'Clever yet kind, that's our Ken,' agreed the happy keepers as they hurried back to their animals, to groom and present them in the best possible light for the delight of the visitors and their children.

Soon everything was in full swing again, with everyone enjoying themselves at the most wonderful zoo in the world. It was as if the brief reign of Stan had never been. As if his bullying manner was no more than a distant dream. For he had grasped his chance and failed. And there was no room for anyone who put themselves above the animals that had found their home in the Last Chance Zoo. Nobody, and never . . .

A Gift for Ken's Zoo

Early one morning Charles the night-watchman noticed a crate outside the gates. In fact, he heard it before he saw it, for it was giving out the most bloodthirsty screams he had ever heard. The plywood crate was about the same size as a washing machine and was pierced with air holes. As Charles warily approached, the screams subsided to low snarlings and furtive scuffles. Scrawled on the top of the crate was a message . . .

A gift for the Last Chance Zoo.

Please give Bruce and Kylie a good home.

Thanks, Ken.

From an animal lover who can't cope any
more.

At once Charles made an urgent mobile call to Ken. The head-keeper was just about to set off on his morning rounds and he was at the gates in less than a minute. Then he and Charles stared at the mysterious crate for a long time, uncertain what to do.

'The crate's quite quiet now, but the screaming was terrible a while ago, Ken,' said the shocked Charles. 'It sounded just like my wife when she blows her top at the kids. She always hugs them afterwards, of course.'

'Bruce and Kylie, eh,' pondered Ken. 'We're obviously dealing with two pets that someone has abandoned. But what kind of pets, I wonder?'

'Well, I must go,' said Charles, glancing at his watch. 'My shift is over – I'm starving for my breakfast and I need a good sleep. But for what it's worth they're probably a couple of puppies that someone couldn't cope with. Though I've never heard puppies scream like that before. Oh well, let me know the outcome, Ken, and I'll see you tonight as usual.'

'Yes, Charles,' said Ken, absently. 'Give my regards to Lady Sarah and the children . . .'

Alone with the gently rocking and snarling crate, Ken put on his glasses and peered through one of the air holes. Fear gripped his heart as he stared inside. In the gloom he could just make out four flashing red eyes and two foaming mouths, each equipped with razor-sharp teeth. In short he was staring at two small killing machines with black stumpy bodies.

Suddenly a clawed paw struck upwards through the air hole sending his glasses flying. It was then that Ken realised he had a problem, or more probably, a major crisis. Quickly he reached for his mobile phone. Even though it was so early in the morning he needed help at once. As he dialled numbers a terrible screaming rent the dawn as Bruce and Kylie gave vent to their rage again.

Hamish the vet promised to come at once. So did the keepers who were still sleeping soundly around the town when they received Ken's emergency call. Totally dedicated to their Last Chance Zoo they didn't even bother to wash as they rushed to obey Ken's urgent summons.

Soon they were gathered around the mysterious crate, wincing as the screams from within assaulted their ear drums. Then they noticed that Ken's large red nose was trickling blood from a vicious scratch. Ken brushed aside their concern and spoke to Hamish.

'Now, Hamish,' he said. 'You're the expert on animals in distress. Take a careful peep inside the crate and tell us what's ailing Bruce and Kylie. And while you're about it see what type of animals they are, for frankly I haven't a clue. But please be very careful.'

Hamish approached the crate and peered gingerly through an air hole. Then, stupidly (for an expert) he poked a friendly finger inside.

'Hello, little mysteries,' he soothed. 'And what might you be?'

Moments later he was reeling back, his finger gushing blood and his face as white as a sheet. The keepers rushed to help him as he collapsed in a heap. They were concerned but also astonished, wondering why he had chosen to become a vet when the sight of blood caused him to keel over in a faint. It was Judy from Exotic Birds who rushed to help him to his feet, wrapped her hanky around his damaged finger and explained to the bemused keepers that Hamish *could* stand the sight of blood, just not his own. She had a soft spot for Hamish and was hoping that he would ask her out for a Chinese meal or something.

In the meantime Ken and the other keepers were pondering their next move. Then Robin from the Snake House came to the rescue. After a quick glance inside the crate he knew what the creatures were. Being an Australian, he recognised the horrible screams of Bruce and Kylie, for while a zoology student he had visited the island of Tasmania. In his mind the contents of the rocking crate was ominously clear.

'We have here two native creatures of Tasmania, Ken,' he announced, looking worried. 'In fact Bruce and Kylie belong to the most feared species of animals on that island.'

'Oh no,' whispered Cathy, biting her knuckles. She had studied the wildlife of Tasmania at college and dreaded the words he was about to say.

'I'm afraid so, Cathy,' said grim Robin. 'Bruce and Kylie are Tasmanian devils, easily the most vicious creatures on earth. I can only advise that Hamish takes them straight to his surgery to put them down with a kind needle.'

'I'll do no such thing!' cried Hamish. 'I'm not

touching those brutes again. You put them down, know-all Crocodile Robin.'

'Coward!' shouted Robin.

'Falling out will get us nowhere,' said Ken, sternly. 'For a start, Bruce and Kylie aren't brutes, Hamish. Bad-tempered they might be, but having been dumped outside our Last Chance Zoo, a chance they will have. We are here to look after all animals as best as we can. So, Robin, what's the natural diet of the Tasmanian devil?'

'Meat,' said Robin, ghoulishly. 'The fresher killed the better. They like to tear at it while their prey is still twitching.'

'Like horrible steaks at a barbecue,' shuddered Sally. 'And folk having to smile while pretending to enjoy it.'

'I mean raw meat,' said Robin, licking his lips. 'That's what the Tasmanian devil loves to munch on.'

'Well, Robin,' said Ken. 'As you know so much about Bruce and Kylie I'm putting them into your care. So get busy and build a secure home for them in your Snake House. And always remember the motto of our zoo. We embrace all animals, no matter what their murky past might be.'

93

'I can just picture it, Ken,' cried Debbie, the zoo artist. 'And I'll help Robin build the perfect home for Bruce and Kylie. I can see a little slice of Tasmania in the heart of England. With a gum tree and perhaps a billabong. I've got a plastic pond somewhere in my studio. And a nice touch would be a fibre-glass kangaroo to make the little devils feel at home. By the way, *are* there any kangaroos in Tasmania, Robin?'

'I doubt it,' said Robin, gloomily. 'If there were, the devils would have eaten them all by now. But I'd like to go and check, Ken. My parents live in Melbourne, Australia, and I haven't been home in ages. Could I take an early holiday and fly back to see them? I could always nip over to Tasmania to find out more about their devils.'

'Chicken,' jeered Tracy of Waterworld. 'Not long ago Ken pinned a medal for bravery on your chest for saving Wayne from Percy the python. I hope that you're not a craven coward deep down. Are you trying to run out as the going gets tough?'

'Pythons and Tasmanian devils are two different things,' snapped Robin. 'Pythons hug, but those devils devour you whole. I want to be alive and in one piece when I accept my next bravery award from Ken.'

'Are you saying that you won't take on the challenge of Bruce and Kylie?' asked Ken, looking Robin straight in the eye. 'Are you hinting that Melbourne and your parents' home will be a refuge from your duty as a keeper at our Last Chance Zoo? I hope you realise that the happiness of Bruce and Kylie is in your hands.'

'Oh, very well,' sighed Robin, reluctantly. 'I'll do it for you, Ken. But if I'm severely injured by those monsters, then I'll know who to blame.'

'We'll call Bruce and Kylie's new home "Devils Corner",' said Debbie the zoo artist excitedly. 'It will be a cosy nook in a corner of the Snake House where everything will remind them of home. Excuse me, but I must dash off to start designing their new abode . . .' and off she went.

Before the morning was out a strong wire cage had been hastily built inside Robin's Snake House. Then, watched by the curious visitors, the crate containing Bruce and Kylie was transported on Ken's fork-lift truck to the Snake House.

In the meantime, Debbie had been busy. Helped by Patsy she had turned the bare cage into what she imagined a small slice of Tasmania would look like. They had carpeted the floor with imitation grass and gladioli flowers. They filled the small billabong with water, fringing its surrounds with empty beer cans and a cardboard gum tree. Debbie had wanted to add a fibre-glass kangaroo, but that would have to wait until she found the time to make it. But the rushed result looked splendidly down under, she thought proudly. She and Patsy had just finished fitting the yellow spotlight to represent the hot Tasmanian sun when Ken and the keepers burst in, dragging the rocking and screaming crate between them . . .

'Open the door of the cage, Debbie,' shouted Ken. 'Then jump back out of danger. We're going to push the crate against the door and open the top to let Bruce and Kylie run wild naturally.'

The instant the top of the crate was opened two black blurs with red eyes and slavering jaws streaked out. Bruce and Kylie immediately went to ground behind Debbie's cardboard gum tree. The terrified keepers slammed the door of the cage and bolted it shut. For about twenty seconds peace reigned in Robin's Snake House.

Then the nerve-jangling screaming began again, even louder than before. Debbie's tree began to sway and thrash as the scufflings of Bruce and Kylie became more demented. The visitors and their children rushed from the Snake House, their fingers in their ears, unable to stand the din any longer.

In a desperate attempt to calm his new charges Robin pushed two pork chops through the mesh of the cage. He nearly lost a finger as Bruce and Kylie dashed from behind the gum tree to seize them, quickly vanishing from sight again. After a minute or two of gnawing and gulping sounds the awful screaming began anew.

'I can't cope with this, Ken,' said Robin, almost weeping. 'The visitors will never come back to see my snakes with that awful racket going on. Just look at Percy and Pandora, all tightly coiled and shuddering. Those devils are driving them mad. Isn't there some way to keep them quiet?'

The ear-splitting screams were beginning to spread like a disease throughout the zoo. It was like a primitive call from the past, awakening the wildness in the breasts of all the animals who heard it. The grins of the monkeys became grimaces as they swung madly on their car-tyre swings, causing the children to shrink away. Even the tame antelopes and goats became butting fiends when the visitors approached to offer them handfuls of succulent green grass or something similar.

And the birds had also caught the fever of distress. Now their friendly calls were shrill and savage as they dashed themselves against the wire of their enclosures.

Yet still the dreadful screaming of the Tasmanian devils went on. By this time Robin was at the end of his tether. Having to cope with his snakes and the little devils was beginning to tell on him. His burden was too heavy to carry and Ken was quick to notice.

'We have a major problem, Robin,' he said, patting the brave boy's back. 'A problem that needs thinking about, and that's what I intend to do.'

'Thanks, Ken,' said Robin, fighting back his tears. 'And don't think I'm trying to win another bravery medal. I just won't be able to sleep at night with the worry of it all.'

Back in his office Ken pondered the problem. Through his window he could hear the shouts of the angry visitors, threatening to stay away from their favourite zoo if something wasn't done about the screaming devils. Ken realised that he had a terrible decision to make. Should he order Hamish to put Bruce and Kylie down in his little Chapel of Rest behind his surgery? Then Ken had a sudden brainwave. Turning to his hotline office phone he dialled a string of numbers. After some crackling noises he finally got through.

'Hello, is that the Tasmanian Zoo?' he said, cocking his ear. 'This is Ken of the Last Chance Zoo. Can I speak to Bob, please? I've got a crisis on my hands.'

'This *is* Bob, Ken,' cried an excited voice from half a world away. 'I'll never forget that I was one of your pupils in zoology college. Your wisdom and guidance steered me through to land my top job in our Tasmanian Zoo. But you'll always be the best head-keeper in the world to me.'

'Oh, I wouldn't say that, Bob,' said Ken, blushing from the other side of the world.

'My mates won't believe it when I tell them I've spoken to you!' yelled Bob. 'They'll be green with envy. So what can I do for you, Ken?'

'Well, it's about two Tasmanian devils that I've taken in,' explained Ken. 'And, frankly, I don't know what to do with them. They haven't stopped screaming since they arrived, and it's upsetting the whole of my zoo. Is there any advice you can give me, Bob?'

'Yes, put them down straight away,' said Bob, briskly. 'Tasmanian devils are more trouble than they're worth. And very ugly little brutes too. Who wants to go to view them in any zoo? Not even in your Last Chance Zoo, Ken.'

'I couldn't do that, Bob,' said Ken, shocked. 'I couldn't order Bruce and Kylie to be destroyed just because they don't fit in.'

'I understand what you mean, Ken,' said Bob. Then his tone brightened. 'But there might be a way to calm those little devils down. A mate of mine made a study of them and he told me a story. It's a long shot, Ken, but here goes . . .'

And he told Ken the story. It was an astonishing tale. Ken began to smile and said that he would certainly give it a go. After promising to send Bob a signed photograph of himself and accepting the offer of a crate of Tasmanian plums for Patsy, he put down his hotline phone.

Soon he was striding from his office to talk urgently with Fiona, keeper of the tarantula spiders. She was known to be a lover of ancient folk music. He quickly explained the situation to her.

'Banjo Billabong, Ken?' she said, amazed. 'Are you a fan of his music too? I've got a rare tape of his songs in my cassette collection.'

'Actually I met him once, many years ago,' said

Ken, remembering. 'So could you bring your cassette to the Snake House as quickly as possible? Because you know that our zoo is facing a visitor crisis, and Robin is close to having a nervous breakdown with the screaming of the Tasmanian devils.'

'All of us keepers are trying to share Robin's pain,' said Fiona, biting her lip. Then valiantly she continued, 'But if my Banjo Billabong tape will solve the crisis then I'll rush it over at once. I'm sure my spiders can look after themselves for a short while.'

The screams of Bruce and Kylie seemed to be shaking the very walls of the Snake House as Ken, Robin and Fiona went into a huddle, trying to make themselves heard above the din. But it was useless, so they resorted to sign language to put Ken's plan into action. Fiona plugged her cassette player into the electric socket and pressed the play button. Immediately the Snake House was filled with the sound of Banjo Billabong singing his famous songs and wobbling his wobble-board while blowing down his didgeridoo. Fiona instantly began to dance and sway in time with the music she so loved, while Robin just looked anxious. Even Ken smiled and snapped his fingers as Banjo chanted the words of that familiar song from down under . . .

Waltzing Matilda
Waltzing Matilda,
Who'll come a-waltzing
Matilda with me?

Suddenly, astonishingly, the screaming stopped. Then from behind the cardboard gum tree sauntered Bruce and Kylie. Their mood was in stark contrast to their former wild behaviour. Their tubby black bodies appeared to be swaying in time with Banjo's music. Fiona was obviously playing their favourite song. Even Robin's pythons seemed to be enjoying it judging by the sinuous curling of their coils.

'Well, would you believe it,' smiled Ken, shaking his head. 'That a song from Mr Banjo Billabong could restore peace to our zoo and save us from possible closure. Keep playing that tape, Robin, and we'll soon be back to normal.'

'I can see another crisis looming, Ken,' said Robin, gloomily. 'Tasmanian Devils are well known for getting bored very quickly. One single tape of Banjo Billabong's songs isn't going to keep them quiet and amused for ever.'

'Fiona,' said Ken, alarmed, 'You're the Banjo Billabong expert. How many songs did he record?'

'Just that one tape as far as I know, Ken,' shrugged Fiona. 'Perhaps he's retired from the folk song scene to raise kangaroos or something.'

'So what happens when Bruce and Kylie get fed up with that single tape?' said Robin, moodily. 'Do we have to go through all the screaming thing again? This is supposed to be a Snake House, not a mental home for demented Tasmanian devils.'

'So we'll need a regular supply of Banjo's songs to keep Bruce and Kylie happy,' said Ken, thoughtfully.

'A constant supply, I'm thinking,' replied unhappy Robin.

'Leave it with me,' said Ken, briskly.

Marching back to his office he pored through his little book of telephone numbers. Then he dialled long distance. A voice answered his call. It was a cheerful Australian voice that Ken had not heard for many years. In the background could be heard the baas of sheep and the moos of cows.

'Good day, Banjo Billabong here,' boomed the cheery voice. 'Who's that, and what can I do for you?'

'This is Ken from the Last Chance Zoo, Banjo,' said Ken. 'I don't know if you'll remember me after all these years.'

'Do I remember you?' cried the delighted Banjo. 'You bet your sweet life I do. I still smile about that time when I came over to visit your zoo, and the incident with your koala bear. The little blighter nearly took my finger off. You certainly take in some wild ones, Ken. And me supposed to be an expert on Aussie wildlife too. How's Patsy by the way? Would she like a crate of my home-grown Victoria pears?'

'I'm sure she'd like that very much, Banjo,' said Ken. 'But to get back to the point of my phone call. You see, we at the Last Chance Zoo have a crisis. I need to know how many Aussie folk songs you've recorded. We have one tape here, but we urgently need more.'

'That's the only cassette I made, Ken,' said puzzled Banjo. 'Then I gave up the music business and bought this sheep and cattle station.'

'Well, I want you to do me a great favour, Banjo,' said Ken, urgently. 'I want you to get back into the recording studio and sing lots more songs. And I'd be grateful if you'd play your didgeridoo and wobble your wobble-board on them. Then I'd like you to send the tapes of the songs to our Last Chance Zoo.'

'Anything for you, Ken,' replied mystified Banjo. 'But will you tell me what this is all about?'

'What's the only way to stop Tasmanian devils screaming?' asked Ken, beginning to laugh.

'I've no idea,' said Banjo, quite bewildered.

'By constantly playing them Banjo Billabong songs,' Ken replied.

'Is that a compliment, Ken?' asked Banjo.

'Of course,' Ken chuckled. 'For what other singer in the world can soothe the savage breasts of the feared Tasmanian devil as well as you? Goodbye, Banjo.'

'Goodbye, Ken,' said Banjo, still bewildered. 'I'll start recording immediately.'

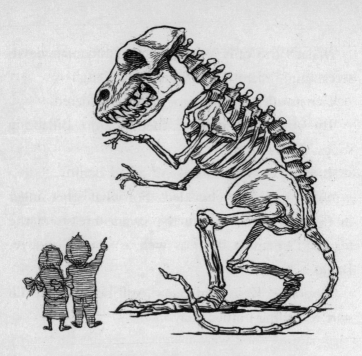

The Ballad of Destiny Dinosaur

There was a large glass and concrete building at the Last Chance Zoo. Inside were the dinosaur exhibits. It was always a cool place to be, even in warm weather, and it was quiet too. Many visitors liked to retreat there, to rest from the hustle and bustle of the busy zoo. But most of them came because of their fascination for dinosaurs.

It was an awesome thrill to be transported back to a time when huge monsters ruled the earth. The building was almost church-like inside. Even loud parents and giggly children seemed to sense the sober mood required as they filed in to view the marvels on display. They were never disappointed by what they saw.

'Just look at the size and the sharpness of those teeth!' whispered a father to his goggling child, pointing to the fossilised jaw of some flesh-tearing creature. 'Who'd stand a chance if cornered by that?'

There were lots of glass cases containing ancient things. They were labelled with dates from impossibly long ago. On the walls hung brightly painted murals, the works of artists with rich imaginations, they were lush with green vegetation, blue seas, and even bluer skies. But central to the pictures were the dinosaurs, fighting and snarling and bloodied and dying. For dinosaurs were always portrayed like that.

There was also a plaster-cast of a huge footprint. It was labelled as belonging to the largest dinosaur that had ever trodden the earth. The children were invited to step inside it, to compare their own shoe-size for fit. There was no comparison of course. Five children could easily fit inside the giant's single step. But it was fun, and it brought home to everyone how truly enormous some dinosaurs had been.

But the stars amongst the exhibits were Destiny Dinosaur and his dad. Their carefully mounted bones took up the whole central space of the hall. Destiny's dad's head reared so high that it almost touched the roof, while, beside him, standing on a craggy boulder and much smaller, was Destiny his son. To the awed visitors it seemed that the youngster was trying to look taller than he really was. Fixed on the boulder beneath Destiny's toes was a brass plaque that read:

> These dinosaurs were dug from the earth and mounted exactly as they were found. Who knows what disaster overcame them millions of years ago? But we know that they died together. What would be their story if they could speak?
>
> I named the small dinosaur Destiny. Perhaps he was a son who died with his father? But why was he standing on a boulder?
>
> Amid such thoughts I donate these precious bones into the care of my good friend Ken and his Last Chance Zoo.
>
> Professor Chuck Redbeard
> Jurassic University
> California

After reading the plaque the visitors and their children would gaze up at Destiny and his dad with great respect or even love. But it was with sadness too that they tried to imagine the dreadful event that had killed the dinosaurs all that time ago.

Some years before, Patsy had pondered on the two dinosaurs, trying to read the story of their fossil bones. Sometimes she smiled and sometimes she wept a tear. Then one day she sat down at her writing desk, determined to tell the tale of Destiny and his dad as she saw it to be. While Ken was patrolling the zoo with his stout stick and torch at night, Patsy would be tapping out words on her typewriter. With passion and love she was writing the Ballad of Destiny Dinosaur.

When it was finished she showed it to Ken who smiled and liked it a lot. So Patsy recorded it on tape, and from that time on the Ballad of Destiny Dinosaur was played in the dinosaur hall every Sunday morning. It became so popular that many visitors made a pilgrimage to attend each week. They came crowding in, some to escape the din of the zoo, others to seek relief from the heat of the summer. But most of them came to sit and gaze at the dinosaurs while Patsy's soft voice washed over them.

There was always an instant hush when the recording began, as adults and children were transported back to experience the short and pain-filled life of Destiny . . .

Destiny Dinosaur worshipped his dad,
He wanted to be like him.
How he wished he could drink all alone a lake dry,
Glare fearlessly into an enemy's eye,
But Destiny's legs and his mouth were too small,
And Daddy was ever so, ever so tall,
So to look a lot older,
He stood on a boulder,
But still barely reached to his daddy's broad
    shoulder.

Destiny Dinosaur, proud of his dad,
So ever so proud of him,
He followed him faithfully on to the plain
Where they stuck in the mud when it started to
    rain.
Small Destiny's dreams on that plain took a blow
As he drowned with his dad when he'd started to
    grow,

With his toes on a boulder,

To look a lot older,

And still barely reaching his daddy's broad shoulder.

Destiny Dinosaur, close to his dad,

So ever so close to him,

For their bones are on permanent public display

And the children who goggle can sense his dismay,

For Destiny's dreams had been nipped in the bud

As he died with his dad in that torrent of mud.

There he stands on his boulder,

Trying to look older,

A little less tall than his daddy's broad shoulder

Then with Destiny's ballad over, the sound of beautiful music swelled through the hall, causing eyes to moisten even more. Soon cameras began to click and flash as visitors jostled to take their close-up snaps of Destiny and his dad. Some children even climbed the craggy boulder to pat Destiny's toes. Then after whispering and waving goodbye, everyone filed out of the hall, leaving the two dinosaurs alone once more. Alone as they had been for millions of years, but always together for ever.

For the visitors it was pleasant to be out in the sunshine again. Their memories of Destiny were already fading as they wandered around the zoo, enjoying the delights it offered. For life was a gift to be treasured while it lasted, and though many of them would return another Sunday to the echoing hall, for now it was forgotten.

Meanwhile, back in that place of ancient things the lights winked out. But still young Destiny would stand on his boulder close to his dad. Never once in his life had he ever deserted his hero. Together they would stay until the end of the world.

Patsy's Christmas Adoption Day

It was nearing Christmas, usually a happy time at the Last Chance Zoo. But recently business had been slow, which was worrying.

It was Patsy who had the great idea. She was in the flat above the office, mending the cracked shell of a turtle named Ocean with super glue, when she suddenly spoke.

'Ken,' she said, 'about our falling attendance figures. Why don't we get the visitors more involved with the animals in our zoo?'

'How do we do that?' murmured Ken. He was painting a penguin's portrait. The bird had a swollen foot and was being treated with Patsy's special ointment. The problem was that the bird was not a good poser and kept waddling back to his bowl of pilchards, just as Ken struggled to capture the curve of his beak in bright yellow paint.

'We could hold a Christmas Adoption Day,' said Patsy, excitedly. 'My plan is to print lots of sticky tickets with the names of our animals and birds on them. Then when the visitors arrive on Christmas Eve, they can choose a ticket for the animal or bird they wish to adopt, insects too, of course. Then they can stick the ticket on the home of their chosen one, to prove that they have adopted them for life. It would also create a firmer bond with the zoo to encourage them to come more often. What do you think, Ken?'

'It's a good idea, in theory,' answered Ken. 'But would it work in practice?'

'Let's give it a try,' urged his wife. 'I'll go and see Debbie first thing in the morning and arrange to print the sticky tickets and the advertising posters.'

'OK,' said Ken. 'I'll discuss the idea with the

keepers on the parade ground in the morning. Actually it's a great idea, Patsy.'

'And the glue has dried on Ocean's shell,' said happy Patsy. 'You can hardly see the join. I'll give him a quick sandpapering and polish before I go to bed.'

'And I'll deliver him back to Tracy of Waterworld tomorrow morning,' said Ken. 'In the meantime I'll get off on my rounds. One of our lions is roaring unusually loudly tonight and I'd better check it out. Let's hope it hasn't escaped and isn't stalking one of Kirk's antelopes. As we know, Kirk would give his life to defend his Game Park.'

Ken threw on his anorak over his pyjamas and hurried downstairs into the cold night air, his flashlight on full beam. There was frost on the ground and the sky was filled with stars as contented Ken made his pre-Christmas rounds of the Last Chance Zoo.

He quickly sought out the roaring lion and settled it down with a juicy steak he had stolen from Patsy's fridge. Then he made his rounds of the other animals, whispering and patting here and there as he fussed over their welfare. Never was there a happier man than Ken as he went about the job he loved deeply.

The next morning on the parade ground Ken told the keepers about Patsy's brilliant idea. They all loved it and were keen to help in any way they could. But they all felt curious about something. Ken had arrived on the parade ground with a laundry basket on wheels. He smiled as he noticed their stares.

'Oh, I almost forgot,' he said, turning to Tracy of Waterworld. 'I've brought back Ocean your turtle, all fit and mended courtesy of the wife.'

'And Patsy's polished him too,' cried delighted Tracy, gazing into the basket. 'Ocean is his handsome self again, and you can't even see the join. Lagoon, his wife, will be so proud and happy, for she's missed him terribly. With his new good looks Ocean will easily win more sticky adoption tickets than any other animal in the zoo. His smart new shell will be plastered with them.'

'Spiders are just as popular,' bristled Fiona. 'Though in a spine-chilling, creepy way, of course. The visitors always make a bee-line for my tarantulas.'

'My tropical birds will outshine the whole zoo,' sniffed Judy. 'They'll be adopted by everyone, mark my words. Especially Testy my parrot, even though he swears a lot.'

'My camels aren't to be sniffed at,' said annoyed Cathy. 'The children love my Crusty's warmth and noble background.'

'You mean they love to spit at him, and be spat at,' grinned Robin. 'My hooded cobra has always drawn much bigger crowds than Crusty. That's because he spits with evil intent. The children know that only the glass between saves them from dropping stone dead. That's why he's so popular. Every child would want to boast that their adopted relative is a spitting hooded cobra. That's why he'll win the sticky ticket contest.'

'Never write off an elephant,' said Bert, wisely. 'They've always been favourites. Every child begs to see the elephants when taken to the zoo. In fact, no zoo could be a proper zoo without them. And there's also the warning that an elephant never forgets. Anyone who didn't vote for them would be a target. My elephants would wait patiently for years and years to get even with the children who refused to award them their sticky ticket, for they never forget an insult.'

'That's just a myth, Bert,' scoffed Sally. 'Everyone knows that monkeys are the bright souls in every zoo in the world. They make everyone laugh. Even their rude backsides are a giggly joy to behold. It's because monkeys remind us of ourselves, I suppose.'

'Not a word about donkeys, I notice,' said Sam, the comic White Rabbit. He began to lead Trigger and Black Beauty away to greet the visitors when the gates opened. 'The kids can't ride a cobra or a tropical bird, but they can always ride a donkey. Come the sticky ticket race, my Trigger and Black Beauty will come in lengths ahead.'

The argument continued, everyone convinced that their own charges would win the most Christmas tickets. Ken tried to calm things down. Then, to his relief, a figure approached. It was Kirk, who always kept himself to himself, but this morning he had decided not to. The keepers quietened as he neared. Everyone was rather wary of Kirk.

Kirk, the keeper of the Game Park, lived a solitary life. His home was a small log cabin he had built amongst the trees of his domain. He was grey-bearded and had large calloused hands. He had always refused to wear his official peaked cap, instead preferring a battered bush hat and khaki shorts which he wore all year round, no matter what the weather.

Ken never chided Kirk about his lack of smartness.

He respected him because Kirk's passion for animals was equal to his own, and that was all that really mattered.

Kirk's section of the zoo was a large area of grassland and woods once owned in richer times by the family of Charles the night-watchman. Roaming freely on Kirk's Game Park were zebras and antelopes, three giraffes, plus two warthogs with a baby on the way. There was also a small lake taken over by the zoo's hippos who constantly churned it into a muddy quagmire with their splashing and wallowing.

Though shy, most of the Game Park animals allowed themselves to be viewed and photographed by the visitors who drove their cars through the park. But the shyest of all were the warthog couple. For complete privacy they had dug a large tunnel into the side of a grassy bank and almost never came out to be gawped at. And Kirk being Kirk, he protected their desire to be left alone, for he preferred a solitary life himself.

'Good morning, Kirk,' chorussed the keepers. 'Long time no see. How's your Game Park? How are the zebras and the hippos? With your permission we'd like to visit them all if we may.'

'Why?' said Kirk, narrowing his blue eyes.

'How are you, Kirk?' grinned Ken. 'I took a stroll through your park last night. I was worried that a lion had escaped and was prowling around for a meal. But thankfully it was a false alarm.'

'I know, I saw you creeping about,' said Kirk with a thin smile. 'I was watching you through my night binoculars.'

'So, to what do we owe this pleasure?' asked Ken.

'I need to see Hamish the vet,' said Kirk. 'I thought he'd be here with you.'

'Not a problem with one of your animals, I hope?' said Ken, anxiously.

'I've got two problems, actually,' replied Kirk. 'Firstly my warthogs are expecting a youngster and it looks like arriving far too early. I'd like Hamish to have a look at the mother.'

'That's wise, Kirk,' agreed Ken. 'And the second problem?'

'The second problem is that Hamish will have trouble trying to examine her. The pair are holed up in a tunnel underground,' explained Kirk. 'It would be far easier if he could examine her above ground. My third problem is . . .'

'You only mentioned two problems, Kirk,'

reminded Tracy. 'I don't think it's fair that you should sneak in a third when Ken is worried enough by the first two. But what is your third problem?'

'This,' said Kirk, wincing with pain. 'I've got this nagging ache in my flank and I'm wondering if Hamish can ease it.'

'You'll find Hamish in his surgery,' said Sally. 'Probably treating a sick animal or peering in his microscope. If you sit patiently and wait your turn I'm sure he'll relieve your pain with one of his powerful medicines.'

'I'll get over there then,' said Kirk, starting to limp away. 'Perhaps he can shoot me with a tranquiliser dart or something.'

'The dart will make your leg go numb,' warned Sally. 'Then you certainly won't feel like dragging your warthogs from their tunnel for Hamish to inspect.'

'We can all help out there,' said Robin, quickly. 'After Ken closes the gates tonight we can go over to the Game Park together and flush out the warthogs, with as little force as possible, of course. That's if Kirk doesn't mind us trespassing on his sacred animal reserve?'

'Sounds fair enough to me,' said Kirk, gruffly. 'So

long as you don't start making regular visits for no reason at all. Having the visitors charging round in their cars is bad enough, without you lot joining in.'

'Your privacy will always be respected by us, Kirk,' promised Ken. 'We'll only be intruding just this once, tonight. And it will be for the good of your warthogs, after all.'

'We could house the warthogs in the stable with the riding donkeys,' suggested Tracy. 'I'm sure that Sam the White Rabbit wouldn't mind. And Trigger and Black Beauty are well known for their mild manners. Then Hamish could visit the expectant warthogs whenever his skills were needed.'

'That sounds all right,' said Kirk, wincing with pain again.

'Before you go off to be numbed, Kirk, there's one more thing,' said Judy. 'We're holding a Christmas Eve adoption event.'

Ken explained Patsy's idea to a very suspicious Kirk.

'But the problem is we don't know the names of your animals, Kirk,' went on Judy. 'So if you could just scribble down their names we'd be very grateful.'

Then she paled as Kirk's bright blue eyes blazed with anger.

'Names?' he roared. 'To insult my animals with names? My hippos are hippos, my antelopes are antelopes, that's name enough for them!' and he turned and limped away to Hamish's surgery.

'We're not offended, Kirk,' cried Fiona after him. 'Ken warned us that you sometimes lose your temper to conceal your really warm heart. We'll just tell the visitors to call a spade a spade when they choose to adopt your Game Park animals. For instance, if they adopt a hippo their ticket will be labelled "Hippo One", or "Hippo Two" and so on.'

'And good luck with the tranquiliser dart,' yelled Tracy. 'We hope that Hamish aims true and brings relief to you.'

As soon as the gates closed that night the keepers got busy. Though it was cold and frosty they refused Ken's offer of overtime, for this was a labour of love. Crusty the camel's old horse box was trundled back into service. With Ken driving and the keepers packed in the back, it was soon parked as close as possible to the tunnel where the warthogs had gone to ground.

Then shouting calming words the keepers tried to coax them out. Their answer was some angry grunting and a brief glimpse of two very ugly faces. Bristly and tusked and piggy-eyed, the warthogs refused to budge from the safety of their home. So everyone was greatly relieved when Kirk arrived from his cabin in the woods. He was leaning heavily on a walking stick.

'You're limping better, Kirk,' said Ken, pleasantly. 'Hamish did the trick then?'

'I won't know till the numbness wears off,' grumbled Kirk. 'I'm sure that Hamish gave me a buffalo shot by mistake. So what are you lot trying to do? You won't move that stubborn pair by cooing at them as if they were pigeons. Open the gate of the horse box then stand out of the way.'

Kirk's numbness hadn't affected his skill with African animals. He began to croon to the warthogs in a strange language, making lots of clicking noises. It was uncanny to watch and listen to Kirk at work with his beloved animals. It seemed that for a while he became a warthog himself. Whatever the language was, it certainly did the trick. A short time later the two warthogs were clattering up the ramp of the horsebox.

'Lovely creatures, warthogs,' smiled Kirk. 'Most people only see the ugliness without, and rarely the beauty within. Now, Ken, I expect you to take good care of them. In the new year I want to see three healthy warthogs enlarging their tunnel in my Game Park.'

'And you will, Kirk,' promised Ken. Then he grinned. 'And I hope that your flank gets better. We wouldn't want Hamish to have to put you down in your prime.'

Meanwhile, back at the donkeys' stable Debbie the zoo artist was putting the finishing touches to her hurried work of art. Helped by Patsy, she had transformed the former dingy shed into a Christmas Grotto. Holly, ivy and silver tinsel now hung from the beams and walls. The only problems were Trigger and Black Beauty. Tired out after their busy day they had slumped down on their familiar bed of hay in the middle of of the stable, braying for their oats and honey supper.

'I'm afraid they'll have to move, Sam,' apologised Debbie. 'I need that central spot for my warthog tableau, and they'll be arriving soon. You'll notice that I've fixed a light to shine down on that very spot, and Trigger and Black Beauty are hogging it at the moment. So perhaps we could make them a warm bed in a corner?'

'So my donkeys take second place to warthogs,'

said gloomy Sam, still dressed in his White Rabbit suit. 'Oh well, if it's so important. But I'll be protesting to Ken about the treatment of my donkeys when I see him.'

So the tired donkeys were moved from the limelight and into the shadows for the time being. But with lots of fresh hay and a bucket of oats and honey the good-natured pair soon settled in their corner.

'And finally we'll check the sound system,' said happy Debbie to pleased Patsy. 'It being Christmas, I'm thinking of playing some nice carols.'

' "Away in a Manger" would be perfect,' said Patsy. 'I've always loved that carol. And I'm sure the warthogs would love it too.'

'What warthog wouldn't?' cried delighted Debbie. Our Christmassy scene is getting more perfect as we speak. Oh, if it would only snow tomorrow. Now that would be the finishing touch!'

There the discussion ended, for suddenly the sound of an engine was heard. It was the horse box squealing to a halt outside the stable. The warthogs and their escort had arrived.

Snorting and tossing their heads the expectant parents clattered down the ramp and immediately made themselves at home in the stable. Cushioned in sweet hay and bathed in soft light the warthogs fell fast asleep to the sound of Christmas carols.

Debbie and Patsy were congratulated for their artistry by Ken and the keepers, and Sam and his donkeys were not left out. All three were patted on the back for making room in the stable for the warthogs. The White Rabbit was so pleased that he did a little jig on his floppy paws and decided not to complain to Ken after all.

'Debbie could make a work of art from an unmade bed,' said Robin, admiringly. 'Which is unlikely, her being so neat and tidy.'

'Here comes Hamish,' cried Judy from Tropical Birds. 'Doesn't he look romantic in his white coat and stern glasses. Now the warthogs are in safe hands as he tends them with his gentle skill.'

'I think I should stay here tonight,' said Hamish after his examination. 'My tests tell me that a birth will soon be taking place.'

'I'll prepare a straw bed for you, Hamish,' said adoring Judy. 'I'll bring you hot coffee and sandwiches to keep you awake through the dismal hours.'

'I'm staying here too,' announced the White

Rabbit. 'If Trigger and Black Beauty are alarmed in the night I want to be here to comfort them.'

'Well done, Hamish and Sam,' said Ken, proudly. 'And everyone else, of course. You're all showing the generous spirit that the Last Chance Zoo depends on. Giving up your plans for tonight to deal with this crisis is much appreciated. In fact I'll be awarding medals to you all quite soon.'

'I was thinking of a little supper party, Ken,' said Patsy. 'I would like to invite all the keepers to our flat for a sandwich and a drink. If they'd like to come, of course. Unless they've better things to do?'

'We'd love to come, Patsy,' chorussed the keepers. In fact they were astonished to be invited, for none of them had ever entered that mysterious flat above Ken's office. It was an honour worth much more than a medal just to peep inside that very private place. And now they were going to.

'Just give me a few minutes to prepare things,' said Patsy. 'Ken will show you up.'

When Ken had made sure that the warthogs were happily secure in the stable, he led the keepers up to his flat. Patsy was waiting at the door. She had changed from her stable clothes into a purple house-coat. She looked regal, in fact she looked uncannily like the Queen with her grey hair and her warm smile. She ushered them in, as kindly as their mothers might be.

The flat was small but cosy. It smelled nicely zoo-like. This was because of the many baskets and cages containing animals and birds that Ken and Patsy were tending and mending. The keepers were soon munching cheese and ham sandwiches and tasting Ken's fig wine made from the crate of figs sent by the Sheik of Araby, Crusty the camel's first owner. In short a good evening was had by all.

True to her vow, Judy used Patsy's kitchen to prepare a thermos of hot coffee and sandwiches for Hamish and Sam the White Rabbit, who were enduring the chill of the night in the stable. Soon it was time for the keepers to return to their homes in the town, to sleep soundly till morning. And it would seem only seconds later when their alarm clocks began to shrill, when it was time to put on their zoo uniforms and go back to work. Not that they minded too much, for they were proud to work at the Last Chance Zoo, easily the best zoo in the world.

It was the morning of Christmas Eve. While Ken was checking out the animals and having his chat with Charles the night-watchman, Debbie and Patsy were pasting up colourful posters around the gates. Then in that bright, though bitter winter morning they set out their stall. Laid out on their table were wads of sticky adoption tickets. All was prepared.

'I don't open the gates until nine o'clock,' grinned Ken, looking at his watch. 'So how about a nice cup of tea? We've got plenty of time.'

'We know our mission, Ken,' said Patsy, firmly. 'Debbie and I are here to hand out the sticky adoption tickets to everyone who enters the zoo. Neither frost nor snow will budge us from this stall.'

Then it was nine o'clock. There was already a queue of visitors waiting impatiently for Ken to open the gates.

'About time too, Ken,' yelled the children as he turned the key in the big padlock.

'Here comes the first wave, Debbie,' cried Patsy, excitedly. 'They've read our posters and now they're rushing towards our stall.'

'Let's hope we're not crushed in the rush,' said happy Debbie. 'And let's hope that we've printed enough sticky tickets to go round.'

'Just keep your nerves, ladies,' soothed Ken. 'Just smile and everything will take care of itself.'

Then his mobile phone began to shrill. Talking

into it he strode away. A problem had arisen in the wolves' den. It seemed they were howling and fighting over their joints of breakfast meat. One wolf had received a much larger joint than the others, and the rest of them didn't like it.

Before an hour had passed the zoo was buzzing with activity. The visitors and their children were hurrying everywhere, slapping their sticky tickets on the homes of their adopted ones. Testy the talking parrot swore roundly as three tickets were stuck on his beak.

Then slowly a rumour began to spread through the zoo. Something strange and special was taking place in a quiet, tucked-away corner. Quite soon the other attractions became deserted. The disappointed keepers noticed that the crowds were heading in one particular direction. Full of curiosity they followed.

It quickly became clear that the destination was the old and sagging donkey stable. They gasped in astonishment to see that the ricketty old timbers were plastered with sticky adoption tickets. A puzzled Fiona peered to read one. It bore a message from a little girl . . .

I wish to adopt the tiny warthog who has no name. Everyone should have a name, so he

will be known as Warty to me, and will be my
brother until the end of our adopted days.

From
Jane, beloved sister of Warty

The doors of the stable had been flung wide open.
Crowds of visitors were jostling to see inside. Framed
by Debbie's soft lighting was a beautiful scene.

On their bedding of hay squatted the warthog
parents, their piggy eyes staring suspiciously at the
sighing onlookers. To one side stood Hamish clad in
his white coat and surgical mask. On the other side
was Sam the White Rabbit, jigging a jubilant dance
of joy. Over their shoulders peered Trigger and Black
Beauty, mournfully braying for their breakfast of oats
and honey, while at the centre of the tableau tottered
a still-wet little warthog, his eyes filled with wonder
and bewilderment as he gazed at the world for the
very first time.

Then from the crowd sounded the voices of the
children singing a song that they had composed from
the depths of their hearts. For they saw no ugliness in
that wrinkled little snout and peering piggy eyes that
gazed back at them. They saw only beauty in that
new-born, innocent form. Full-voiced they sang:

Gentle Warty meek and mild
So we name this new-born child
Born upon a bed of hay
We will love him every day

And as they sang the day passed and the light began to fade. But from somewhere candles were found and lit, casting a warm glow outside the stable to match the light within. And then it began to snow.

'Quite silly,' murmured Ken as he strode away. 'But then zoos are supposed to be silly sometimes. That's why silly old fools like me work in them . . .' and brushing away a tear he straightened his red-banded cap and switched on his mobile phone, ready to respond to the next problem or crisis call that was bound to occur before he closed the gates of the Last Chance Zoo for the night.

As darkness fell the snow piled thicker. And outside in the brightly-lit town the bells began to ring out for Christmas.

Bruno's Picnic Spree

Bruno had always been an adventurous bear cub. Once he had fallen from the top of the tree stump in his compound and had broken his nose. Hamish the vet thought Bruno was a very lucky bear. He said that had he fallen on his head he would have been seeing double for the rest of his life.

Hamish straightened Bruno's nose and slapped an elastoplast on it. But as the cub was still very groggy after his accident, he was taken in to be fussed over by Patsy in the flat above Ken's office.

Bruno soon became addicted to the high teas that Patsy laid on. He especially enjoyed her salmon sandwiches and strawberry ice cream. In short, Bruno was living like a little king.

But noses heal, and so did Bruno's. He was returned to the compound, back to the care of his anxious parents, to become a normal bear cub again. However, Bruno was unable to settle back into his old life. He badly missed the high teas that he had enjoyed in the flat above the office. And this was why Sam the White Rabbit was phoning Ken urgently one busy Saturday morning.

'Ken, Bruno has escaped from his cave in his compound,' he shouted. 'And he's here at the gates as bold as brass, sniffing the picnic baskets of the visitors. He's the centre of attention, and it isn't fair. Not a single child has giggled at my White Rabbit suit, or my giant pocket-watch. And my donkeys are still waiting for customers to ride them. Bruno is stealing my show and I could weep, I really could!'

'Can you capture Bruno and hold him until I arrive?' questioned Ken.

'It's too late,' wailed Sam. 'He's vanished into the crowd of visitors. He could be anywhere at the moment. And my donkeys are stamping their hooves in anger because they're being ignored.'

'Calm down, Sam,' soothed Ken. 'I'll sort this crisis out. I'll make an emergency announcement over the public address system. We'll soon have that bear cub rounded up.'

A few moments later the zoo's loud-speaker system crackled into life.

'Good morning, visitors,' boomed Ken's voice. 'This is your head-keeper calling. Don't be alarmed, but a bear cub has escaped from his family compound and is roaming at large in the zoo. Here is his description. He has silky brown fur and lemon-coloured eyes, and answers to the name of Bruno. When you have your picnics on the grass, check who's sitting beside you, because it might be Bruno, who has no permission to be out and about on his own. As for further clues, he loves salmon sandwiches and strawberry ice cream. If anyone spots him, please shop him at once. It won't be grassing because it's for his own good, and his parents are very worried about him. So please report all sightings of Bruno to the keepers. Thank you, visitors. This is Ken saying over and out, and wishing you all good bear hunting.'

Almost at once reports began to come in of Bruno being spotted at various places around the zoo. The first report was from Tracy of Waterworld.

'Ken,' she cried. 'I've had a Bruno sighting. He was seen helping to carry a family's picnic basket down to my beach. Then before he could be arrested he had rifled their basket and had scoffed the apple pie that the children had been looking forward to. Now the children are crying and their parents are complaining, and I don't know what to do.'

'And where is Bruno at this precise moment?' asked Ken, urgently.

'I don't know,' wept Tracy. 'He's just melted into the crowds again. No doubt in search of another picnic basket to plunder. In the meantime, these parents are complaining about being mugged by Bruno the bear and they're even demanding compensation!'

'Offer them free hot-dogs, Tracy,' ordered Ken. 'And all the ice cream they can eat. Our visitors must not be upset.'

'I'll do that, Ken,' said Tracy, signing off weepily.

Throughout the day more Bruno sightings were reported to Ken's office. It seemed that the small brown bear cub was appearing everywhere at once. According to reports he had gate-crashed every picnic that had taken place, and all at the very same time, which was impossible of course. The greedy cub's plan seemed to be to find a picnic, scoff the lot and then move on at top speed to find another victim. Despite Ken's marches around the zoo he always seemed to be a picnic behind the elusive Bruno. Some children proved awkward when he questioned them.

'Yes, a small brown person did share our picnic basket,' said one boy, cautiously.

'And where did he go afterwards?' asked Ken.

'I'll never grass on Bruno,' the boy yelled. 'Go and track him down yourself, Mr Head-Keeper.'

As the day wore on Bruno still remained uncaptured. Ken was frustrated by hoaxes and red herrings everywhere he went. He began to have doubts that Bruno had escaped at all. So he went back to the bear compound and checked it out. But sure enough Bruno was missing. The worried looks of his parents were proof enough of that. So where on earth could the missing cub be?

Then finally the day was over and the visitors went home, tired but happy after their visit to the Last

Chance Zoo. As Ken locked the gates he was confronted by an angry White Rabbit and two mournful donkeys.

'Thanks to Bruno our day was completely ruined, Ken,' complained Sam. 'Not a single soul wanted a ride around the zoo while that bear cub was on the rampage. I've been in show business all my life, but I've never been upstaged by a bear.'

'But where is he?' asked Ken, bewildered.

'How would I know?' shrugged the White Rabbit, leading Trigger and Black Beauty back to the stable for their supper of oats and honey.

Back in his office, Ken tried to puzzle it out. Then suddenly he heard a 'whoofing' sound from the flat above. Climbing the stairs he cautiously opened the door.

The scene that met his eyes was extraordinary. On the living-room carpet was spread a checked table-cloth. On it was a large plate heaped with salmon sandwiches. Beside the plate was a tub of strawberry ice cream. Squatting side by side and tucking in were Patsy and Bruno. For a while Ken just stared, his anger rising. Then Patsy noticed him.

'Hello, Ken,' she smiled. 'Bruno was scratching at the office door so I invited him up. Come and sit down and get something to eat before our guest eats it all.'

'Bruno,' said Ken, sternly addressing the bear cub. 'Do you realise the chaos you've caused in the zoo today? Like stealing food from picnic baskets and making children cry? Well, you must be punished for your escapades. Starting tomorrow you'll begin a punishment diet of bitter berries and water, with no sweet treats to follow. And you'll also be put under house-arrest in your family cave in the compound until you have learned your lesson. And why you want yet more food after all you've stolen is beyond me.'

Bruno completely ignored Ken's threats. He continued to scoff down salmon sandwiches between pawfuls of strawberry ice cream, uttering whoofs of pleasure between gulps and burps.

'I don't understand, Ken,' said smiling Patsy. 'What's that about Bruno roaming about and terrorising the zoo all day? He came to visit me early this morning and hasn't left the flat at all. I thought I'd prepare this special high tea to remind us of the times we spent together when he broke his nose.'

'So what bear cub has been vandalising the zoo all day?' Ken demanded to know. 'Every report I received fitted Bruno's description exactly. And he certainly hasn't got a twin brother.'

'All rumour, Ken,' said Patsy. 'And you know how rumours spread.'

'So that's your and Bruno's story, and you're both sticking to it,' Ken smiled. 'Oh, well, there's no real harm done. And what has the suspected bear cub got to say for himself?'

The only reply was more whoofing noises as Bruno scooped another dollop of strawberry ice cream from the tub.

'Come and sit down and enjoy our picnic,' urged Patsy. 'You need to relax after spending your day chasing invisible bear cubs.'

Grinning, Ken kicked off his shoes and sat cross-legged beside them. For a while he was certain that his wife and Bruno were winking at each other, but Ken had decided to let the matter rest. All in all it had been an especially exciting day at the Last Chance Zoo. With their hands on their hearts not one visitor and child would have denied that. Of course, Ken was not fooled for a moment. He was too clever a head-keeper to be taken in so easily.

'Hey, leave me one of those salmon sandwiches,' he protested as Bruno stretched out his paw for more.

But the greedy little bear easily beat Ken to the plate
and scoffed the lot.

The Mystery of the Missing Duck

One morning before he opened the zoo gates, Ken called Tracy of Waterworld into his office. His normally smiling face was stern, which made Tracy a bit nervous. Like all the other keepers she did her work as well as she could, and happily. For working for Ken was an honour, and a few words of praise from him were much prized, so seeing him looking so grave disturbed her. Sitting her down he gave her a mug of tea, and then the questioning began.

'Did you count your Siberian ducks this morning,

Tracy?' he asked gently. 'Because during my dawn stroll down to your lake I counted only five.'

'You mean six, Ken,' said Tracy, firmly. 'All six were happily swimming in circles when I left to go home last night.'

'Well, there are only five now,' said Ken, shaking his head. 'Have you any idea what could have happened to number six?'

'I hope you're not accusing me of murder, Ken,' cried Tracy. 'I had a Chinese take-away for my supper last night. I've never tasted duck in my life.'

'Of course I don't suspect you,' soothed Ken. 'Everyone knows how much you love the birds and animals in your care.'

'Perhaps the missing duck went for a midnight swim all by itself,' said tearful Tracy. 'They do sometimes. Perhaps it's fast asleep in the reeds somewhere.'

'I'm afraid not, Tracy,' sighed Ken. 'I tramped around the lake and poked all through the reeds with my stick, but there was no sign of that missing duck number six.'

'I think I know the answer,' said Tracy, inspired. 'Our Siberian foxes. It makes perfect sense. Siberian foxes love to eat Siberian ducks. And you know yourself that the fence around the fox enclosure needs mending. As I see it the duck went for a solitary swim and was ambushed by a fox who had squirmed out through a hole in the fence.'

'Good thinking, Tracy,' mused Ken. 'Before I open the gates I'll check the foxes for any suspicious evidence. In the meantime, keep a close eye on those five remaining ducks, for you know how rare they are.'

A while later Ken arrived at the Siberian fox enclosure. As he gazed through the fence, the three foxes stared insolently back at him. They looked cunning, furtive and guilty. But then all foxes do, for being foxy is the name of their game. Yet as Ken looked around he could see no evidence of the missing duck. The foxes had no feathers clinging to their muzzles, and there was no scatter of bones to suggest that a murder had taken place. He came to the conclusion that the foxes were innocent. After apologising for doubting them, Ken marched away to open the gates and let the visitors in. Then he returned to his office to puzzle and think.

His thoughts were interrupted by the ringing of his phone. It was Charles the night-watchman. He had finished his night duty and was back home in his cottage enjoying a hearty breakfast.

'Hello, Ken, I forgot to tell you something early this morning,' he said, cheerfully. 'Everything is arranged for Friday night.'

'What's arranged?' said puzzled Ken.

'Surely you haven't forgotten,' chided Charles. 'It's your wedding anniversary on Friday. Sarah and I have arranged a dinner for you and Patsy at the cottage.'

'Oh yes,' said Ken, absently. 'Patsy did mention some such thing.'

'So, we'll expect you Friday night then?' said Charles. 'Sarah is planning something special.'

'That's nice, Charles,' replied Ken. 'Friday night it is. Goodbye.'

But Ken's thoughts were elsewhere as he sat in his office and pondered the missing Siberian duck. Where could it have got to, he worried.

Tracy of Waterworld was also having problems. Some of the visitors were dismayed to see only five Siberian ducks instead of the usual six. They took out their annoyance on Tracy. How could she lose such a rare duck, they complained. She was supposed to be saving the wildlife of the planet, not mislaying it.

Later that day Tracy had an upsetting incident with some school children. A week before they had visited the lake to draw portraits of the Siberian ducks swimming on the water. Today they had returned to colour in their sketches.

'Hey, Miss,' a small boy shouted to Tracy. 'I've coloured in five ducks but I can't colour in number six.'

'Why not?' said Tracy, all agitated.

'Because number six is missing,' said the boy.

'Just use your imagination,' snapped Tracy, close to tears. 'Siberian ducks all look very much alike.'

'Not in the changing light, they don't,' said the stubborn boy. 'All ducks are different because of the sun and shadow bouncing off their beaks and feathers. Our art teacher told us that. I suppose I'll have to leave duck number six blank. But it will spoil my picture, Miss.'

'Just do what you think is best,' said Tracy, controlling her temper.

It was easily Tracy's worst day as a keeper at the Last Chance Zoo. Everyone was blaming her for the mystery of the missing duck. Yet how could she be expected to watch over her charges twenty-four hours a day? She had a private life of her own after all. It was so unfair. And wasn't Charles the night-watchman supposed to be patrolling the zoo through the night? Had Ken questioned Charles about the missing duck? It was just as well that Tracy loved her Waterworld job. Otherwise, for two pins she would have packed her rucksack to go hiking in Snowdonia.

By Friday morning there was still no sighting of the missing duck. Even Ken had given up on ever seeing it again. It was very sad, but life at the zoo had to go on. Throwing bread to five rare ducks instead of six was better than throwing no bread at all. And there were lots of other attractions around the zoo, plus hot-dogs to eat and donkeys to ride.

Then came Friday evening when Ken wished the visitors good night and locked the gates. Now it was time for him to go back to the flat and get ready for the planned dinner with Lord Charles and Lady Sarah.

Ken looked very smart in his best suit, with his grey hair neatly combed. Patsy had insisted that he leave his red peaked cap at home. After toasting Ken and Patsy with a glass of wine, Sarah went into her kitchen to bring in the food. First she carried in bowls of good, plain vegetables that she grew in her small garden. Then triumphantly she bore in a roasted duck on a silver platter, drenched in rich orange sauce.

Charles the smiling host began to carve the succulent bird.

In those moments Ken's faith in human nature sank to an all-time low. How he got through that meal he did not know. How could his friend Charles brazenly carve up a rare Siberian duck before his very eyes without a flicker of shame? And then the dinner party was over. After polite good nights Ken and Patsy walked home to their flat.

'I'd never have believed it of Charles,' said Ken, sadly. 'To think that a duck could ruin our long friendship.'

'It was a beautiful duck,' said Patsy, puzzled. 'And Sarah cooked it perfectly.'

It was clear to Ken that Patsy wasn't thinking what he was thinking. She could see no connection between the missing Siberian duck and the duck they had just eaten. So he didn't press the matter. But he intended to have a serious talk with Charles when they met at the gates the following dawn.

Ken's face was stern the next morning. Charles was perplexed. He had never seen his friend in such a mood before.

'Charles,' said Ken, 'you know that our zoo has lost a rare Siberian duck. Can you throw any honest light upon the matter? Because during our dinner party last night I—' and that was as far as he got. For he was suddenly interrupted by a voice. It was the jubilant voice of Tracy. Ken was surprised to see her up and about so early. He noticed that she was carrying a plastic shopping bag with air holes punched in the sides. And the bag was squirming and quacking.

'I've found our missing Siberian duck, Ken,' she cried. 'Instead of going out clubbing last night I went on a detective search. And guess where I found this little fly-away-from-home?'

'Surprise me, Tracy,' said Ken, as pleased as Punch.

'Floating on the local duck pond with some new-found friends,' giggled Tracy. 'Mostly common ducks, but with two minder swans sailing on either side. My guess is that our duck decided to fly back to Siberia but ran out of puff, so it flopped into the local pond to get its breath back. Which is where I tracked him down and popped him in this bag.'

'You're a credit to our zoo, Tracy,' smiled relieved Ken. 'Remind me to award you a medal for your dedicated work.'

'We're all pleased, Ken,' said Charles, though he still looked puzzled. 'But what were you about to say before Tracy arrived, about me throwing some honest light on the subject of the missing duck? You weren't accusing me surely?'

'Of course not, Charles,' said Ken, embarrassed. 'I'd got this silly idea in my head but it's gone now.'

'I'll get off home then,' said Charles, happy again. 'I'm starving for my breakfast. And Sarah will bawl me out if my fried eggs go rubbery. By the way, Ken, I've got another duck hanging in my garden shed. My cousin in Scotland sent me down a pair. So how about another dinner again on Sunday night?'

'Patsy and I would be delighted,' grinned Ken. 'And may I say that the duck Sarah cooked for our wedding anniversary was delicious.'

'Yes, and nowhere near as tough and stringy as Siberian duck is said to be,' said Charles, mischievously. 'That had been on your mind, Ken.'

'Sorry ever to have doubted you, Charles,' said Ken.

And they parted as the friends they had always been.

'And now to deal with you two,' said Ken, turning back to Tracy and her quacking plastic shopping bag. 'First of all we must get that duck back to the lake to bond with his family again. As for you, Tracy, when we assemble on the parade ground for smartness inspection I want you to step out of line for a special purpose!'

'You aren't going to sack me, Ken,' cried Tracy, distressed. 'I couldn't help losing the duck but I did hunt him down again.'

'And I'm very proud of you,' said Ken, kindly. 'Now get that duck back to his family and don't be late for parade.'

An hour later a moving ceremony took place on the small parade ground, just before Ken opened the gates of the zoo. Adjusting his red peaked cap, Ken gravely approached nervous Tracy and pinned a Dedication to Duty medal on to her lapel. The other keepers cheered and clapped which made Tracy blush. Her award also made them feel hopeful for themselves, for they knew that Ken had lots more medals in his desk drawer. To be honoured by the greatest head-keeper in the world was something they all yearned for. Perhaps one day it would be their turn to stand on the parade ground and receive a medal from Ken.

Then just after closing time that evening Tracy ran sobbing to Ken again. Calming her down he managed to get some sense from her.

'Another of my Siberian ducks has gone missing, Ken,' she despaired.

'Surely not the same one,' said Ken, bewildered.

'I wouldn't know,' wept Tracy. 'They look so alike you see.'

'It's the call of Siberia, I suppose,' sighed Ken. 'But don't worry yourself, Tracy. The little rascal is probably hiding in the reeds somewhere. We'll flush it out. For none of our six ducks could possibly fly all the way back to Siberia.'

'It could be floating on the local duck pond as the other did,' said Tracy, hopefully. 'With common ducks for company, and stately swans as escort.'

'Who knows the mind of a duck,' smiled Ken. 'Especially the mind of a Siberian one. Now get off home and stop worrying. We'll have the problem solved tomorrow morning, just you wait and see . . .'

Who would want to be head-keeper of the Last Chance Zoo with all the worries the job entailed? Ken would. That's why he did it, and loved doing it too.

Testy's Tangled Love-life

A favourite character at the Last Chance Zoo was Testy the talking parrot. Lots of visitors, especially children, made a point of calling in at Judy's Exotic Bird House to hear his latest insults and swear words. It was well known that he was taught swear words by the children who whispered them into his cocked ear. Some days he became addicted to a certain phrase. A particular one was taught to him by a girl named Rachel who had fallen out with her best friend Sally.

'Sally's got a big bum,' he squawked over and over, bouncing up and down on his perch. Though it made the visitors laugh, Testy soon dropped it. Anyway, the insult was out of date because Rachel and Sally were soon best friends again. But Testy returned to swearing, uttering ever more shocking words. He loved to shock; being shocking meant being noticed, and he loved being the centre of attention. In quiet moments Judy would smack his beak and scold him, and Testy would bow his brightly coloured head and look ashamed. For some time afterwards he would shuffle along his perch and preach at the visitors.

'Swearing is wicked, swearing is bad, if you don't stop it Hamish will put you down,' he would screech at anyone who approached him. But he soon returned to his old ways.

'Kevin's got a snotty nose,' he screamed.

'Excuse me, Miss,' said Kevin, approaching Judy. 'I haven't got a snotty nose. I always use a handkerchief. It's my sister who's been spreading that rumour, just because I read a lot and I'm good at maths. Will you please shut Testy's beak before I shut it for him?'

'I'll try,' said Judy, despairing. 'But you know

what he's like when he gets a phrase stuck in his head.'

'Ben wets the bed,' yelled Testy.

'I really don't know what to do with him, Ken,' said desperate Judy to the head-keeper when he popped in one day. 'Popular though he is, he does upset some of the children with his rude remarks.'

'We'll soon have a solution to that problem,' said Ken, confidently. 'What Testy needs is the company of a fellow parrot. And she's arriving today.'

That afternoon a large cage was delivered to the Last Chance Zoo. Inside was a very pretty lady parrot named Tessa. She had been put into the care of Ken's zoo because she had problems. All her life she had been haughty and coldly silent. Other zoos she had stayed at complained that she was a bad mixer and spent most of her life gazing into space. When she was released into Testy's roomy cage, he fell in love immediately. But the lady spurned him. She kept to her side of the perch and with a few angry pecks made sure that Testy kept to his. The visitors declared that Testy and Tessa looked a perfect couple, but they were wrong. While he was loud-beaked and noisily cracked his seed, she daintly nibbled hers. In fact they were as different as chalk and cheese in every respect. It seemed that Testy's attempt to begin a love-match was heading nowhere.

So Judy their keeper stepped in. She began to whisper words into Testy's ear. He was a quick learner.

'Tessa is a pretty girl,' he screeched when the visitors approached their cage. They all agreed, though Tessa herself remained silent.

'Testy is a handsome boy,' he squawked, which was true. But there was still no response from Tessa.

So Testy went back to swearing again, and now the object of his bitterness was the lady Tessa who continued to ignore him.

'Tessa's got a big bum,' he yelled.

This was quite untrue, but the visitors and their children encouraged him to say even more outrageous things.

'Tessa's got a snotty nose,' he shrieked to all and sundry.

'And you've got a foul beak,' said the small boy named Kevin, tapping the cage. He had also been insulted by Testy on numerous occasions. 'In fact, a nasty swearing beak.'

'Kevin is a specky four-eyes,' taunted Testy.

'But I'm very clever,' said Kevin. 'Which is more than you are. No wonder Tessa wants nothing to do with you. I'm also polite. That's why I've got a girlfriend and you are all alone.'

Testy's reply was a stream of swear words that made everyone blush. His hot temper soon made him the talk of the zoo.

Meanwhile Tessa remained aloof. She wanted nothing to do with a parrot who let his loud beak rule his heart. Sometimes the feathers would fly if the lovelorn Testy sidled too close to Tessa's side of the perch. Despairing, not knowing what to do, Judy phoned Ken.

'I've got trouble in Exotic Birds, Ken,' she said. 'And I need your help.'

'Is it a problem, or a full-blown crisis?' answered Ken. 'Only at the moment I'm dealing with the ring-leader tarantula spider who's escaped again. He's trying to organise a mass break-out.'

'It's Testy and Tessa, Ken,' wailed Judy. 'If Tessa attacks Testy much more he'll have no feathers left.'

'I'll be over as soon as I've recaptured the ring-leader tarantula,' replied Ken, briskly. 'Just try to stop any more feathers flying until I get there.'

Half an hour later Ken marched into Judy's Exotic Bird House. Watched by a crowd of sympathetic visitors she explained the desperate situation. The floor of the parrot cage was a sea of scattered seed and feathers – Testy's pecked-out feathers. He now had a bald spot on his head where Tessa had given him a good beaking. He crouched on his side of the perch looking very sorry for himself. Tessa was as far away from him as possible, her usual aloof self.

Ken walked across to the cage and began to whisper in Testy's ear. At once the unruly parrot was alert and listening. Then Ken moved to talk softly into Tessa's ear. For the first time at the zoo she began to show interest. Then Testy spoke.

'Tessa hasn't got a big bum,' he squawked.

'And who's got a big swearing beak?' cajoled Ken.

'Testy has,' came the shrieked reply.

'And what has Tessa got?' asked Ken.

'Tessa's got a little bum,' yelled Testy.

Ken's magic with his animals was amazing. Testy seemed to be a completely changed bird. And all for the love of Tessa who began to cast him admiring looks from her side of their perch. Then Ken put into Testy's beak a large succulent nut. Warily Testy shuffled along the perch and offered it to Tessa. She accepted it and ate it in her dainty way.

'And what will we never do again?' asked Ken, sternly.

'We'll never swear again,' screeched Testy.

Kevin, the small boy who had been abused by Testy's language, was amazed. He so admired Ken that he decided at that moment to become a head-keeper of a zoo, hopefully the Last Chance Zoo. He reached up to stroke Testy's balding head.

'Kevin is a specky four-eyes,' yelled Testy. 'And Judy has a big bum.'

Ken smiled as he marched away. He knew that things would now be well in the Exotic Bird section of the zoo. The love-match between Testy and Tessa had begun, and would one day bear fruit. And Kevin was not at all offended by Testy's 'specky four-eyes' insult. Neither was Judy much bothered by his 'big bum' remark, for she had always been as slim as a reed, and knew that Testy said outrageous things just to be noticed. And now he had been noticed, by the classy Tessa no less. But he would always get the urge to swear from time to time. But then he was a parrot after all.

'Miss,' said Kevin, 'when Testy and Tessa have

chicks could I have one to wear on my shoulder like Long John Silver?'

'Of course you can,' smiled Judy. 'But rather you than me. The swearing in my ear would be unbearable . . .'

The Sad White Rabbit

Sam the White Rabbit took his comedy very seriously. For years he had greeted the visitors at the gates of the zoo in his fluffy costume. He would pretend to be very worried as he ran around tapping his outsize pocket watch and muttering about being late for a very important date. His act always made everyone laugh, even those who had seen it many times before. His frantic cavorting had never been copied by Trigger and Black Beauty. They were calmness itself as they plodded around the Last

162

Chance Zoo with the children playing cowboys and Indians on their backs. Sam never joined the other keepers on the parade ground in the mornings. He needed to be at the gates early with his donkeys, brushing their manes and tightening their saddles in preparation for the morning rush.

'Anyway,' Ken would smile, 'who can tell whether a white rabbit is smartly turned out or not?'

It was strange, but no one seemed to know anything about Sam when he shrugged out of his rabbit suit at the end of the day. During zoo hours he was the ever-funny bunny, capering along beside his donkeys and worriedly tapping his plate-sized pocket watch. But when the day was done and his costume hung up, he became almost a stranger to his fellow keepers. After feeding his donkeys their buckets of oats and honey and bedding them down for the night, he would vanish into the town.

Then one day Black Beauty collapsed and died while plodding home from work. Hearing the dreadful news Ken and the keepers gathered in the stable to comfort a mourning Trigger and the weeping White Rabbit.

From that time on, Sam changed. Gone was his funny act at the gates in the morning. No longer did he check his large watch for lateness. Now he and Trigger were forlorn figures as they went through the motions of entertaining the visitors. It was plain that their zest for life had vanished with the death of their beloved Black Beauty.

Ken and the keepers watched all this with mounting concern. One night after the gates had closed they met to discuss the problem.

'I saw Sam leaving the stable a few minutes ago,' said Cathy. 'He just murmured goodnight and hurried on by. I've never noticed before how thin and lonely he looks out of his rabbit suit.'

'Even when dressed as a rabbit he no longer skips, but barely drags his paws along the ground,' said Robin, shaking his head. 'It's so tragic him losing Black Beauty so unexpectedly.'

'And painful for Trigger too,' said Cathy. 'That poor donkey must be very lonely in his stable without company.'

'I wonder what Sam is doing now?' said Bert. 'He always was a loner. We've worked together in this zoo for many years, and I can't say I've ever known him. Inside his rabbit costume he was the joking character that everyone loved, but outside it he has always been withdrawn.'

'And now he's a sad White Rabbit trying to cope with his grief,' said tearful Sally, 'in charge of sorrowful Trigger who clops around the zoo with his chin on the ground. What can we do to help them through their misery, Ken?'

'What if we hugged Sam every time we saw him?' suggested Fiona of the spiders. 'And Trigger too, of course.'

'Actually, Patsy and I have been discussing the problem,' said Ken. 'I think we might have a solution.'

'We're all ears, Ken,' said Cathy, brightening. 'Anything that will make our White Rabbit and Trigger happy again.'

'Well, as you know, Black Beauty was laid to rest behind the stable,' said Ken, 'beneath her favourite apple tree. But there's no headstone to mark the passing of that faithful old donkey. So Patsy and Debbie have designed a fitting monument to her. And I'm going to award Black Beauty a Long and Faithful Service medal, which will be fixed on her headstone to remain for ever. What do you all think?'

'I think it's an absolutely wonderful idea, Ken,' said Cathy, mopping her weeping eyes.

'What an honour,' whispered Fiona. 'To be awarded a special medal in death from Ken's desk drawer. Black Beauty will surely rest in peace now.'

'The ceremony will be held on Sunday morning,' said Ken. 'Sam always enters the stable at eight o'clock in order to get ready for work, so we'll need to get there much earlier. Before he arrives we must have Trigger saddled and waiting at Black Beauty's graveside. Then, when Sam sees the headstone and the medal on the plaque, we can only hope that it cheers him up a little. Finally, and most importantly, no one must breathe a word to Sam about the surprise that's waiting for him.'

'Not a single hint, Ken,' promised the keepers. 'Such a good idea deserves to be kept secret till Sunday.'

It was Saturday morning. Down at the gates the White Rabbit was trying to be cheerful for the sake of the children. But they knew he was very sad over the loss of Black Beauty, and they understood because they missed her too. Trigger was not forgotten either. He was patted constantly and fed chocolate and apples, which he chewed in the most mournful way. Instead of riding him around the zoo, they thought it was more respectful to lead him along the route by his bridle. With the White Rabbit trudging along behind it looked like a funeral procession, as perhaps it was.

Throughout that day the White Rabbit was too down-hearted to notice the activity of the children. They were shaking rattling tins in the adults' faces, and the smiling parents were popping coins into the slots. And all the while the children were whispering excitedly amongst themselves. It was as if they had a secret they were determined to keep from the White Rabbit.

Though they were itching to tell, not one child blurted a word to him as he trudged dejectedly around the zoo behind Trigger. The secret would remain just that until the time came to reveal it.

The keepers were also watching their words when they met the White Rabbit that day, for they had their own secret to keep. Only Fiona almost let the cat out of the bag when she gave him a knowing wink as he passed, which puzzled him, but only for a moment. The truth was he was much too down in the dumps to really care about anything at that time.

And then it was seven o'clock on Sunday morning.

The keepers had all arrived at the zoo especially early. While Patsy and Debbie erected the beautiful headstone on Black Beauty's grave, the keepers fed Trigger his oats and honey breakfast, and then fitted on his freshly polished saddle and harness. Then he was led out to stand beside the grave beneath Black Beauty's apple tree.

At exactly eight o'clock Sam arrived for work for he was very punctual. It was only when he changed to become the White Rabbit that he always seemed to be late. He was surprised to see Ken alone in the stable, with no sign of Trigger. But before he could speak Ken was gently leading him around to the back of the stable. And then Sam saw . . .

The grave of Black Beauty was heaped with piles of beautiful flowers. Grouped around were the keepers, all smiling, but not too broadly on this serious occasion. And beside the magnificent headstone stood Debbie holding Trigger's bridle. He was softly braying, his nose snuffling amongst the flowers. On the headstone were engraved the heartfelt words:

Here lies Black Beauty, deeply mourned
by Trigger, the White Rabbit

and all their friends at the
Last Chance Zoo.
We will all remember you,
dear Black Beauty

Beneath the words was a simple cross set into the stone. It was the medal that Ken had vowed to award her in death. After gazing and reading Sam broke into tears. He was quickly surrounded and comforted by his friends the keepers. After a while Ken interrupted the scene.

'Come, Sam,' he said, gently. 'We need our jovial White Rabbit back. I'm sure that he and Trigger would hate to be late for a very important date. So what do they plan to do this Sunday morning?'

'We're going back to work, that's what,' cried Sam. 'Let's go and get those gates open, Ken. Come Trigger, old friend, we've got lots of entertaining to do!'

There was another big surprise waiting for the White Rabbit and Trigger at the gates of the zoo. Drawn up at the entrance was a horse box surrounded by a crowd of cheering children. When the White Rabbit and Trigger appeared, the door was thrown open and the ramp lowered. Down it came clattering a jet-black donkey. Two small children led it forward.

As the strange donkeys sniffed each other's muzzles, and as the White Rabbit looked on in delighted astonishment, the small girl spoke.

'Dear White Rabbit,' she said, shyly. 'We the children are very sad about Black Beauty. So we've collected lots of money to buy a new companion for you and Trigger. Her name is Black Bess and we hope she will become a friend and a part of your funny act. I'm sure that she and Trigger will get along, for her favourite meal is a large bucket of oats and honey.'

The White Rabbit was too overcome with emotion to reply. He simply took the bridle she handed him in his white paw. Then the small boy spoke.

'Could I ask you a favour, White Rabbit?' he said.

'Of course,' whispered tearful Sam through his buck-teeth and whiskers.

'Can I have the first ride around the zoo on Black Bess?'

And then the crowd around the gates broke into laughter and applause as the White Rabbit began to scamper around on his huge, floppy paws, frowning and tapping his outsized pocket watch. For suddenly he seemed to be running late again. Late for a very important date with happiness in the future.

Ken's Wonderful Day

On the first day of June a letter arrived for Ken. It was a very special letter because it was embossed with a royal crown, which could mean only one thing. Ken was being honoured by yet another foreign king or prince. Every country in the world respected and honoured Ken for his dedicated work at the Last Chance Zoo. Every country on the planet that intended to set up a zoo always asked for his wise advice.

'Open it then,' said Patsy, impatiently. 'And if it's

from our friend the Sheik of Araby tell him that I don't need any more figs for the moment.'

Ken opened the letter and began to read. As he read he began to blush. By the time he had finished reading, his neck and ears were as crimson as his nose and cap. Silently he handed the letter to Patsy. Her face was a study of astonishment and pride as she whispered the opening words.

'Hearing about the wonderful work you do with animals, Her Majesty the Queen is pleased to confer on you a knighthood. Her Majesty will visit your zoo on the first day of July to present you with the said honour . . .'

Quite stunned, Patsy gave the letter back to her husband. Then looking him up and down she said, 'You'll need a new cap of course. And a tidy haircut. And I want you to wear all those medals that you've been awarded from all around the world. It's about time I got them out from my cabinet. And you'll need to practise bowing, and I'll need to practise my curtsy.'

'I still can't believe it,' said Ken, shaking his head.

'Well, I can,' said Patsy. 'And it's not before time in my opinion.'

'Well, knighthood or not, I've got work to do,'

said Ken, putting on his red cap. 'I've got the keepers to inspect and the gates to open. Then I intend to have a few words with those idiot suppliers. Fancy sending three cases of frozen fish-fingers for my penguins. Are they completely mad?' and he marched down the stairs and on to the parade ground to inspect the patiently waiting keepers.

He said nothing to them about the royal letter. But later that day Patsy did, for she was proud of Ken, and why not? Soon all the keepers and the visitors were gossiping about the news, and saying how well deserved Ken's knighthood was.

'To think,' said awed Tracy, 'the Queen is actually coming to our zoo to dub Ken with her silver sword! She must be very anxious to meet him.'

'Perhaps she's having trouble with her corgis,' grinned Robin, 'and is in desperate need of advice from Ken.'

'Tracy is being serious,' snapped Judy. 'Please keep your crude Australian jokes to yourself.'

'I think it's right that Ken should be honoured by the highest person in the land,' said Fiona, with feeling. 'Patsy told me that she has a cabinet filled with dusty medals awarded from around the world that Ken never wears. She said that he's spent his whole zoo life hiding his light under a bushel. In fact his shyness gets her down sometimes.'

'Well,' said Bert, a firm royalist, 'on the first day of July Ken will be forced from under his bushel. For Her Majesty the Queen has commanded it!'

'What a lovely moment it will be,' said Sally, dreamily. 'Ken kneeling, and Her Majesty tapping his shoulders with her sword and saying, "Arise, Sir Ken". She *will* say that, won't she?'

'If she doesn't then it would be an insult to our Ken,' said Cathy. 'And the Queen would never insult the best head-keeper in the world, because she's got perfect manners.'

They were still talking about the great day to come, and the parts they would play in it, as the sun went down. How should they reply if the Queen spoke to them, and what if their mouths went numb and dry? Then Ken came marching up. He had just closed the gates and was on his way back to the flat to enjoy the fish and chip supper that Patsy had promised him.

'What are you lot plotting?' he said. 'Have you no homes to go to, no parties to attend?'

'Why didn't you mention the first of July, Ken?' accused Debbie. 'Why did you leave it for Patsy to tell us?'

'It slipped my mind,' said Ken. 'Anyway, there's no rush. It's still a month away.'

'A mere month!' cried Debbie. 'Do you realise how long it will take me to design all the artwork, and the flags and bunting to make our Last Chance Zoo a fit place for the Queen to visit?'

'Debbie's right, Ken,' said Robin. 'There's an awful lot that needs to be done in the next few weeks. For a start my Snake House could do with a lick of paint.'

'I only got the official letter this morning,' protested Ken.

'Which you could have read out on the parade ground, but didn't,' said annoyed Debbie. 'It shows a lack of consideration, Ken.'

'I'm sorry,' said Ken. 'I'll make it official now. On the first of July the Queen is coming to visit our zoo.'

'To dub you a knight, we know that,' snapped Sally. 'We had to learn it from Patsy. And what will you be wearing on the big day? You'll certainly need a new cap and a proper haircut. Patsy also said that you've got a cabinet filled with awards and medals that you never wear. So do you intend to come out from under your bushel and wear them?'

'Patsy would be pleased if you did,' persuaded

Judy. 'She's started dusting and polishing them in preparation. And we'd all be very disappointed if you didn't wear them on the big day. We're all very proud of you, you know.'

'OK, I will,' sighed Ken. 'Now, can I go and enjoy my fish and chips?'

'You can, Ken,' said the keepers, 'now you've made the promise to wear all your medals on the big day.'

At last the great day arrived and the Last Chance Zoo was spick and span with fresh paint. The animals were also looking their best, all groomed and bright eyed for Ken's big day. The gates were a riot of flags and bunting as Ken marched down to open them. He looked magnificent in his best uniform, with his chest glittering with medals awarded by the many zoos around the world. Grinning broadly he flung open the gates to the cheers of the waiting crowd. Then began the rush inside to secure the best ringside seats around the small parade ground where the ceremony would take place. Just before twelve o'clock it was announced over the loudspeakers that some very important visitors were about to arrive.

The keepers was standing in a semi-circle on the

parade ground, the medals that Ken had awarded them glinting in the sun. Just in front stood Ken, with Patsy beside him looking regally beautiful in her long dress. Soon the encircling crowds broke into cheers and waved their flags as a fleet of shiny cars purred in through the gates.

The largest and shiniest car came to a stop exactly beside the small red carpet that Debbie the zoo artist had so carefully laid. Then out stepped the Queen to frenzied applause, plus a gasp of surprise from the crowd. For the Queen looked almost exactly like Patsy, the wife of their beloved head-keeper Ken. Both of them had lovely grey hair and warm smiles. The Queen walked along the carpet to greet the bowing and curtsying zoo staff. Then she addressed Ken.

'And you must be the famous Ken,' she smiled, shaking his hand. 'I've heard so much about the good work you do. I understand that your Last Chance Zoo is world renowned, as you are. I'm delighted to meet you.'

Then she greeted Patsy. The Queen had a bemused look on her face as they shook gloved hands. It was as if she was trying to remember where she had seen Patsy before. Then the Queen's husband shook hands with Ken.

'You must know a lot about animals,' he teased. 'You've got more medals than me. Tell me, what do you know about toads? Would you say that Stan was a fitting name for a toad?'

Whatever else was said was drowned by a trumpet fanfare from the town band. This was to herald Ken's knighting. When the brassy blaring had stopped, the Queen was handed a beautiful silver sword. Ken knelt on his lion-taming chair, which Debbie had covered in blue velvet. The Queen tapped him gently on each shoulder with the sword and gave him a warm smile.

'Arise, Sir Ken,' roared the crowd, enjoying every moment of the historical event. 'Arise, our Knight Ken, the best head-keeper in the world!'

Then the band began to blare again as the Queen began her walkabout. The crowd pushed and shoved to present her with flowers, all received with a gracious smile. Then away from the bustle, Her Majesty was able to view the zoo in peace. She seemed to like all the animals and the birds, and even the tarantula spiders, for she smiled at every one. But she kept her distance from Crusty the camel.

'I know *him*,' she said. 'He was a gift from the Sheik of Araby. Unfortunately we had no room for him at the palace. And he could be very messy with his spitting.'

In the meantime the Queen's husband was poking gentle fun at Ken's many medals, demanding to know where each one came from.

Then the ceremony was over and the shiny cars purred away down the drive of the Last Chance Zoo. After the crowds had gone and the gates were locked the keepers gathered to discuss the day's exciting events. Amongst them was the newly honoured Lady Patsy, who took their teasing in good part. Then she said goodnight and left.

'Where's Sir Ken?' grinned Robin. 'He's noticeably absent. Is he now too proud to mingle amongst us humble serfs?'

'But didn't he look noble kneeling on his velvet chair,' said Debbie. 'And the Queen didn't trip over on my red carpet because I laid it very carefully.'

The keepers could have stayed talking all night, but a voice interrupted them. It was Ken, just down from his flat, stick in one hand and flashlight in the other.

'We were just talking about your wonderful day, Ken,' said Cathy, 'and how proud we are of you. Your rows of medals looked very impressive.'

'And they're all going back into the cabinet where they belong,' said Ken, gruffly, 'for will one of them ever save the tusk of an elephant or the horn of a rhino? Anyway, goodnight to you all. I'm making an early round of the zoo tonight. All the day's happenings are bound to have upset some of our animals.'

'Goodnight, Sir Ken,' chorussed the keepers. 'Happy prowling!'

And they all parted to go their separate ways until the morning brought them together again.

Later that night Ken met Charles down by the gates. Charles had a strange story to tell.

'Ken,' he said, 'I've heard all about animals escaping from zoos. But would you believe that I saw a black panther digging under the wire to get inside ours? It must have been one of those large cats who are rumoured to be living wild in the countryside. Anyway, I bedded it down in the lion enclosure and fed it.'

'Well done, Charles,' said Ken. 'For we've never turned an animal away from the Last Chance Zoo. We'll have another talk about it in the morning. In the meantime I'm going to get some sleep.'

'Goodnight, Sir Ken,' said Charles, grinning.

'Goodnight, Lord Charles,' replied smiling Ken. And they parted.

And so ended another beautiful day at the Last Chance Zoo, easily the best zoo in the world.

Another Hodder Children's Book

THE ARK OF THE PEOPLE

W. J. Corbett

THE FIRST STORY IN THE ARK OF THE PEOPLE
SEQUENCE

In their ancient oak the miniature Willow People live in peace and harmony with nature. But humans flood the valley.

In a desperate bid to survive, the People set sail in an oak-bough Ark. Somewhere beyond the floods is a new life for them, a new home. They will need all their courage to find it.

But they have also saved Deadeye of the Nightshade Clan and his host of vicious allies. Now it is more than courage they will need . . .

madabout**books**.com

. . . the

Hodder Headline

site

for readers

and book lovers

madabout**books**.com